The
Chinese
Fire Drill

The
Chinese
Fire Drill

Les Roberts

Five Star • Waterville, Maine

Five Star First Edition Mystery Series.

First Edition, Second Printing.

Published in 2001 in conjunction with Tekno Books and Ed Gorman.

Set in 11 pt. Plantin by Minnie B. Raven.

Printed in the United States on permanent paper.

Library of Congress Cataloging-in-Publication Data

Roberts, Les.
        The Chinese fire drill / Les Roberts.—Five Star 1st ed.
        p.   cm.
        ISBN 0-7862-3760-0 (hc : alk. paper)
        1. Hong Kong (China)—Fiction.   2. Missing persons
—Fiction.   3. Novelists—Fiction.   I. Title.
        PS3568.O23894 C47 2001
        813'.54—dc21   2001051240

For Holly

Chapter One

I've seen too many movies.

Or written too many, I can't decide which.

In Hollywood movies we've always been led to believe that the Pacific Rim, or what we used to call the Orient (before it became inexplicably rude and un-PC to do so), is a place of strange and mysterious goings-on, with beautiful sloe-eyed women slinking around in cheongsams and sinister little men selling opium or military secrets.

It was also a place few of us ever expected to go, before Vietnam and television and the Internet turned the whole world into a global village and Americans were popping off to Bangkok or Singapore for a romantic week or weekend.

Yet I found myself in Hong Kong not too long ago, doubly surprising since the colony, which used to belong to the British, reverted to the People's Republic of China and is now behind the Bamboo Curtain.

But that's what you do for friends.

I was close to finishing up a novel. That's not exactly hard news—I'm always working on a novel. That's what I do. It's what I love to do. I sit down at my word processor and indulge my imagination all day long, creating amazing adventures and exotic settings and steamy terrific sex, and my publisher sends me money.

It's like stealing.

I get to feeling guilty about how easy it is sometimes— usually once a year on a rainy Tuesday in February. I manage to live with the guilt until the mood passes.

Anyway, sometime during the middle part of the morning I heard the phone ring but didn't answer it. I never answer the phone before three o'clock in the afternoon because that's my writing time. Besides, I know my Thai houseboy will pick it up after the second ring and take a message that occasionally proves decipherable. His name is Piyawadee Chitbangonsyn, but he prefers being addressed as Bill. And that's a good thing, because if he wanted me to call him Piyawadee Chitbangonsyn I'd probably fire him and have to answer my own telephone. There are some who might think it exotic to have their own houseboy, but when you live in a huge wooden bungalow overlooking the biggest klong in Bangkok like I do, it doesn't seem unusual at all.

Except for his coming into my study with a fresh pot of coffee I rarely see Bill at all during the day. But on this particular morning he knocked, seeming terribly excited about the phone message he had taken for me. Bill tends to get excited about a slight change in the direction of the wind, so I was prepared not to take him seriously, but after a protracted conversation with him and a careful perusal of the name and number he had scrawled on the margin of my daily newspaper, I figured out the call had probably come from Jake McKay in Hong Kong. He had called and left a message the night before, too, but when I get into one of my writing frenzies towards the end of a book I don't see anyone, call anyone, get drunk, make love, go to the beach, watch television, or behave in any other manner that might be considered human.

That may account for my two broken marriages back in Los Angeles and a pathetic array of aborted relationships all over the world.

Jake McKay was one of those people I listed under the very sparse heading of Real Friends. If you don't know the name Jake McKay, you'll know the face, seen in more than a hundred movies dating back to the sixties, when he always played The Kid, the rookie cop or the still wet-behind-the-ears soldier who always got himself killed while clutching a letter from his mom or a photo of his best girl. Along the way he'd become a fine actor. Refreshingly, he'd always refused to take his career seriously and had remained a real person through all of it, even the Best Supporting Actor nomination. Once back in Los Angeles, before I'd relocated to Thailand, he'd called me for lunch and I'd said, "You're the only actor in town who wouldn't have mentioned you were guest-starring on *ER* tonight," and he'd answered, "Why in hell would I do that? I called you for lunch, not to give a press conference."

Jake was a rarity.

After the nomination, which he didn't win but was proud of anyway, Jake had opted to take life a bit easier and began globe-trotting, eventually settling in Hong Kong in a large, well-appointed flat overlooking Repulse Bay, and when the colony reverted from British to Chinese rule in 1999, he saw no reason for making a change. He invariably worked in every film shooting in Asia, usually cast as a hard-bitten correspondent or smuggler or Interpol cop now that he'd gotten older and more weathered.

I admired Jake McKay for many things—his talent, his lifestyle, his humor, but mostly for his capacity for friendship.

I tried several times to reach him later that day, only to be told by the Chinese operator that no one was answering, which I had already figured out for myself. It wasn't until the next morning that there was an answer at his flat. It was not Jake who answered, however, but a lady with a low, mellow baritone voice and a delightful British accent. When she heard my name, she told the operator she would take the call.

"Mr. Holton," she said, "this is Katherine Longley. I'm Jake's flat-mate."

Good old Jake, I thought. I tried to picture the face that went with that voice. It was a very good face I imagined.

"Jake tried to phone you several times."

"I know. I couldn't get back to him until now. Is he there?" I hoped he was; transoceanic phone calls were too expensive just to chat with strangers, even ones with low, liquid voices.

"No," she said. "He's disappeared. It worries me. There's been some kind of trouble. I don't know what it is, he wouldn't tell me. But I know that's why he wanted to contact you."

Adrenaline raced through me and I got that fast, tingling feeling on the skin of the backs of my hands, the same sensation I always experienced when I changed freeway lanes and narrowly missed hitting another car. The one-word summary, I suppose, would be fear, and the realization that we're always only an eyelash-flicker away from disaster, no matter how resolutely we take our vities and floss after eating and wear our galoshes in the rain.

"What do you mean, disappeared?"

"I haven't seen him since early yesterday morning."

"Well, I wouldn't worry about it too much, Miss Longley. Jake has been known to get—sidetracked."

"Not this time. His boat is missing, and he was sure it had been stolen."

"*The Hong Kong Lady*?" I said. "He loved that boat."

"He was most upset about it, as you might imagine." God, I love the British talent for understatement. "He'd been to the authorities, he'd made inquiries, and then yesterday morning he went out and I haven't seen him since. He was supposed to meet me for a drink in Central at five o'clock, and he never arrived or rang up. That's not like Jake."

"I agree. Is there anything I can do?"

Fear and hope and hesitancy made her voice even lower. "I do know Jake was going to ask you to come here. He said you were the only one he knew who could help him. 'Anthony Holton will figure this out,' is what he said."

"I'm very flattered. But I don't know what I could do. I'm a novelist, not a tracer of lost persons."

She didn't say anything for quite a while, and her silence earned the phone company an awful lot of my money. It also worked on my conscience; Jake was my buddy, and he'd be there for me if I needed him.

"Look, Miss Longley," I finally said, guilt getting the better of my good judgment, "I'm not going to be able to get out of here until later this evening. That will get me there after midnight. Will that be all right?"

"Oh, that would be super," she said. "Jake said he'd pay for your ticket."

"We'll worry about that later. I'll see you tonight."

"Good. I'll pick you up at the airport."

"Fine. I'm forty-eight, six foot five, with white hair . . ."

"I know what you look like," she said. "I've seen the photos on your book jackets. Jake keeps them all on a special shelf, rather like a holy shrine. He's terribly proud of you."

"That's because I'm the only literate friend he has."

"You're a good friend, Mr. Holton."

"I try to be, Miss Longley."

After I hung up I dug my passport out of the junk drawer where I keep important papers like that, glumly regarding the photograph which didn't flatter me at all. The photographer had insisted I smile, and when I smile in photos my gums show. I didn't know how long I'd be away so I packed for a week-long trip, figuring I'd have a few jackets and a suit made while I was there. That, after all, is what people do in Hong Kong.

I'd first met Jake McKay several years before. I was a Hollywood screenwriter at the time, and had penned an epic about the Vietnam War that had been optioned by a fly-by-night independent film company. The producer had made a deal with the government of a little country in Southeast Asia called Cheung Dong to shoot the entire picture there, Vietnam itself being less than hospitable to American film companies in those days and the Cheung Dong currency comparing favorably to the U.S. dollar. Jake, a bit long in the tooth to be playing The Kid anymore, was cast as the megalomaniac infantry colonel, and we became best friends the moment we looked at one another.

During the thirteen weeks of filming, almost twice what the producers had estimated and budgeted for, Jake and I spent our days bitching about the rigors of location shooting and our evenings getting quietly drunk in the local hot spot on beer that resembled cat piss in both color and taste, and on their own house brand of bourbon seemingly flavored with vintage basketball shoes.

While we were shooting the combat scenes in the northern part of the country, an army of rag-tag revolutionary zealots carrying Chinese rifles and surplus Soviet grenade launchers stormed the tiny capital some forty miles to the south, eliminated the prime minister and his cabinet in one savage public execution, herded all the citizens not wearing red armbands into concentration camps, and Cheung Dong became the People's Republic of Cheung Dong. Overnight a new country was born, an entire nation of human beings was plowed into the swampy muck of the delta, and a Hollywood movie shoot was shut down in mid-schedule. Most of us didn't get paid, but we figured we were lucky to be getting out of Cheung Dong at all.

My only previous close-up exposure to tragedy was witnessing a six-car pile-up on the San Diego Freeway, so I was profoundly moved by the coup that had occurred under my very nose. I headed back to California where I sat down and wrote a novel based on my experiences. *The Fall of Cheung Dong* was quickly snapped up by a major publisher, became a Book of the Month Club alternate selection, and to my astonishment walked away with that year's Pulitzer Prize.

Since Hollywood regards a Pulitzer as the equivalent of an honorary doctorate from Slippery Rock State Teacher's College, i.e. nice enough but meaningless at the box office, I jumped into the world of books with both feet and began writing action-suspense novels set in Asia. The P.P., as I always refer to it, assured healthy advances and book club sales for all my subsequent work; I turned my back on the movie business altogether.

And since my second divorce coincided with my third week on the best-seller list, leaving me with no Los Angeles ties except the guys from the morning coffee-klatches at Nate and Al's, I decided to make a lifestyle change. I moved to Bangkok, where I now reside in comparative luxury in a three-bedroom home with a live-in houseboy and an *amah* for what it would cost me to rent an efficiency apartment in Santa Monica. I love my house, which hangs over the Grand Canal, and if occasionally I look up from my writing to see a dead dog floating by in the softly eddying current, it's a small price to pay.

Jake McKay, on the other hand, had been bitten by that strange bug which often attacks visitors to the Far East, and had chosen Hong Kong. We usually visited each other's bailiwicks at least once a year for a few weeks of camaraderie and pub-crawling, so I knew Hong Kong pretty well and had several acquaintances there, even though my work had kept me from visiting Jake for the past eighteen months or so.

When Bill heard where I was going, he fussed at me like a Jewish mother, and at the airport pressed into my hand a small travel kit laden with Kaopectate, Tylenol, Listerine, Band-Aids, and a silver flask filled with my favorite Bombay Sapphire gin, as though I were embarking on a solitary trip through Antarctica instead of to one of the most cosmopolitan cities in the world.

But Hong Kong could be an easy place in which to get into trouble. Even in the midst of its twenty-first century sophistication, a respected and prominent citizen could become a missing person amongst a population of more than four million.

No different than any other big city, I suppose—except that this particular missing person was Jake McKay. And he was my best friend.

Chapter Two

My flight was an edgy time for me, brooding as I was over Jake's possible fate. I kept telling myself he had simply gone on some sort of marathon debauch, and that when I arrived he'd be waiting for me at the airport with a chilled Pouilly-Fuissé. But it was difficult maintaining that happy fiction when I realized *The Hong Kong Lady* was gone. Jake had bought the boat shortly after his resettlement in Asia and he took the same kind of pride in her that antique car buffs exhibit toward their Bugattis, beaming like a new father as he extolled the wonders of her burnished teak railings and gleaming brass fittings.

It is no small matter to steal a forty-foot boat. One doesn't slip it surreptitiously under a jacket or into the lining of a trench coat. Having successfully negotiated its theft, one doesn't hide it in the back of the closet behind a pile of dirty shirts, or stash it in a locker at the bus station. And one wouldn't haggle over the disposal of a stolen yacht in a dim-lit bar or on a street corner or even at a pawnshop. One must have a hiding place in mind when stealing anything that size—and a purpose.

Jake McKay was no dummy; he could figure that out as well as I. And so he went off looking for his *Lady* and now he, too, was missing.

It's a lot easier finding a hiding place for a person rather than a boat, even if his face was familiar to anyone who had gone to a movie or watched TV for the last thirty years. I tried not to think about those hiding places—the shallow grave just off the highway, the bottom of Hong Kong Harbour with a few concrete blocks for weight, or the barren hills of the New Territories, between Kowloon and Mainland China.

I felt almost human by the time the plane touched down, but I stepped off with rubberized knees anyway. Kai Tak airport is located in the northeast corner of the Kowloon Peninsula, and its runway is accessed via a terrifying swoop over some low-lying hills and then onto a long, skinny spit of spill and concrete stretching out into the ocean. Many airborne agnostics revert to the religions of their childhood when approaching Kai Tak, and pray themselves down. I slipped back into the devout Catholicism that I had abandoned in early adolescence and beseeched God for a safe landing. I shouldn't have looked out the window—big mistake.

There was no mistake about Katherine Longley, however. She was tall, with light brown hair that looked windblown; later I came to realize it looked that way by design. To meet my plane she had chosen a gray skirt that showed off sleek, stockinged legs, and a white blouse with a mauve sweater thrown over her shoulders, its sleeves carelessly knotted together beneath small breasts. She wasn't beautiful, but she was very attractive in that way of some women who had grown into their looks so that at thirty-five or so they knew exactly who and what they were and were comfortable with it.

Her handshake was firm and warm and definite, and only a small frown line between perfect, full eyebrows betrayed the worry she was feeling over Jake.

And then there was that voice, telling me how good it was of me to have come on such short notice. I've always wanted someone with a high-class British accent to tell me it was good of me to come. Through all my worries over Jake's safety, I found myself envying him, because this was the kind of lady not often found in Los Angeles show business circles.

"You must be exhausted after that long flight," she said after I had cleared customs, a procedure that takes less time in Hong Kong than anywhere else in the world, as though it was inconceivable that anyone would attempt to smuggle something *into* Hong Kong. She led me to her car, a bright red Nissan sports car, and we were out of the airport in no time.

"I've reserved a room at the Conrad International," I told her.

"Oh, no," she replied. There was simply no question about it. "You're coming back to the flat."

"I don't want to crowd you."

"Nonsense. You'll stay in Jake's room."

I blinked and remained silent. The entire concept of Jake having a separate room was one I'd have to try to assimilate.

"When he returns," she continued, "we'll see to putting you elsewhere."

Again there was that flinty determination: "when" Jake returns, not "if." I liked that.

We drove through the near-deserted streets of Kowloon, silent and slumbering after midnight. Except for the tourist areas, Kowloon resembled a sleepy Midwestern city. There was a slight mist, rendered other-worldly by the modern orange-yellow street lights—very cinematic. When we emerged from the long, dark tunnel that snakes beneath Victoria Harbour, connecting Kowloon, on the mainland, with the island of Hong Kong, we were in Causeway Bay, much more lively with its cluster of shops and restaurants and clubs.

"Really," I said, giving it one more try, "I'll be lots less trouble at a hotel."

"You'll be no trouble at all. Besides, the Conrad International is clear on the other side of the island from us. Jake isn't there, of course, and Boomer hardly ever is."

"Boomer?"

She shrugged. "Repulsive name, isn't it? Boomer Crane. Our other flat-mate. You might even have heard of him. He was some sort of big football player back in the U.S., he tells us."

I hadn't heard of him, but then I can count on the toes of one foot the number of football players I *had* heard of.

Katherine steered the Nissan expertly through serpentine streets that were all one way and all seem to go in the same direction, past the fabled Noonday Gun near the Causeway Bay Typhoon Shelter, and then northward, up over the breathtaking Victoria Peak on which the city of Hong Kong is built. By craning my neck behind us I could see the lights of the Central District; from the top of the peak their high-rise buildings and apartment blocks looked like a well-done cardboard mock-up, one of those greeting cards that are packed flat and then spring into three dimensions when opened.

I had to hang onto the dashboard and pray some more as Katherine descended to the southern side of the island where Repulse Bay looks out over the South China Sea. She wasn't exactly reckless, and she seemed to know what she was doing, but she seemed to be taking the downward curves with an abandon I might have found fascinating were I not white-knuckle terrified.

To distract me from the thought that I was hanging perilously over the edge of a cliff, I decided to proceed with my investigation right here.

"Was Jake working on a picture, Ms. Longley?"

"Kate," she corrected, tires squealing around a mountain curve. "He hadn't done a film in about four months, but he was getting ready for one about smuggling in the Far East. He told me he had an awfully good role in it and that they were going to pay him a lot of money."

"Who's they?"

"He, actually. An American named Averell Brown. He's some sort of important Hollywood producer."

I frowned, trying to recall Averell Brown. Of course, a producer needs no degree, no resume, no union card to hang out his shingle. He simply goes to Kinko's and has business cards made up saying he is a producer, and the more easily led tend to believe him.

Financially speaking, there are two types of assets—solid and liquid. In Hollywood there's a third kind: gaseous. More simply put, hot air. I wasn't going to put Averell Brown in that category just yet, but I was hard-put to remember a single film or TV show he'd had anything to do with.

"Does this Brown have the money to do a big-budget film?"

"From what Jake said, he's doing it with Hong Kong money. Someone here is funding the film and Brown is personally producing it. There's been talk in the local papers mentioning Tom Cruise, among others. Jake was to play one of the bad men."

That sounded a warning bell. If you're going to sling bullshit, you might as well use the biggest name you can think of. "Is Brown in Hong Kong now?"

"Yes," she said, "for several months. He lets an expensive house on the mid-levels with his wife and a couple of live-in Chinese servants. He spends lots of money, and does it rather conspicuously. Mr. Brown is a bit hard to digest sometimes . . ."

"How do you mean?"

"He's very obnoxious to be with. He's loud and demanding and rude. He thinks he owns everything he puts his hands on."

I laughed. "You've just described the quintessential Hollywood producer."

"I suppose," she said. "He's a bit different, though. He's been involved in a lot of things—at least that's what the gossip is. Smuggling, et cetera . . ."

"Anyone else Jake bummed around with?"

She laughed, like clear, cold spring water tumbling over a large stone. "You know Jake. He was everyone's chum."

"Anyone more than the others?"

She hesitated just a hair longer than she should have before she said, "A journalist named Stanley Nivens. He's with Reuter's."

I looked over at her. In the darkness it was hard to tell, but it appeared that the knot of muscle at the base of her jaw was jumping just a bit. I decided to find out more about Stanley Nivens.

"What made him different? To Jake, I mean?"

"Oh, Stanley's a lot of fun," she said in a tone that let me know he was no fun at all. "He hasn't drawn a sober breath in years. He could charm a stone wall. He's been in Asia too long, I'm afraid, and it's begun to get to him."

"In what way?"

She didn't answer, and the resolute fashion in which she stared through the windshield at the road told me she didn't intend to, either. I let it go.

"Forgive me for being personal," I said, "but I'm having some trouble sorting out the sleeping arrangements at your place. You said I'd be staying in Jake's room. Aren't you and Jake . . . ?"

It broke the tension. Her laugh was lusty and full-throated, throwing her head back and arching her long patrician neck. "You don't know the realities of living in Hong Kong," she said. "It's an island, and there's no place to build suburbs. So real estate here is as expensive as any place in the world. Rentals are obscene. So our flat costs over nine thousand a month U.S. Jake asked Boomer to move in and share the rent with him about a year and a half ago. I joined them eight months later at considerably reduced rent because I do most of the cooking. We're all friends, and we're flat-mates, and that's all."

"Makes economic sense," I said, "but there's not much privacy to do your own thing."

"The privacy issue hasn't come up," she said, pronouncing privacy the British way with a short *i*. "Jake does all his nonsense on the boat, and Boomer is around so rarely that it isn't a problem."

I wanted very much to ask her where she did her "nonsense," but I wisely shut up and watched ahead of us until I could see moonlight toe dancing on the water of Repulse Bay.

Then I said, "Where is Boomer when he's not at the flat?"

"Manila," she said. "Bangkok. Singapore, Kuala Lumpur. He travels all through Asia. He's in export, like me. But I'm just an office drudge."

I nodded. "What else has Jake been up to? Any business deals? Romances? Visitors?"

"Apart from acting, Jake's principal business seems to be pleasure," she said. "I suppose he has investments somewhere, but I don't know about them. As for romances, Jake is never lonely, but I've never known him to be really involved with anyone. More than three times to bed seems to be a meaningful relationship for him. And visitors? I'm not sure I understand."

"Out-of-town visitors," I said.

"Rather a constant flow. Mostly film people, but no one who stayed more than a few days, and then it's usually just a meet for drinks and dinner. Gene Hackman was through about a month ago."

I nodded. Jake and Hackman had done a film together very early in both their careers.

"Oh, and of course the yacht race."

I turned in the seat to look at her. "Considering Jake's yacht was stolen, I might like to hear about that."

She was too involved with the road to give me an icy stare, but her tone was cool. "I'm not used to this, Mr. Holton. Clues and motives and people disappearing. I'm just telling you things as they occur to me."

"Sorry," I said. "Tell me about the yacht race. And please call me Anthony."

She took a breath and settled down. "It's an annual thing from here to Manila. Jake's competed for the last three years. Last year he finished fifth, and this year—the race was about six weeks ago—he came in second. He was very proud, as you might imagine."

"Did he have a crew?"

"Boomer. And Jake's boat boy, a young Chinese named Johnson Lau. He looks after several boats besides Jake's, but when the race comes round he always sails on *The Lady*."

We were coming out of the mountain pass and into Repulse Bay with its high-rise apartments, shops, restaurants and, incongruously, the golden arches of Mickey D's.

"That extraordinarily ugly building over there," Katherine said, pointing, "is the most expensive residential property on the island. Because of the view. But once upon a time that was the site of the Repulse Bay Hotel. Elegant.

Old-world. Every time you walked in there you expected to see Somerset Maugham sitting in the lobby." She shook her head sadly. "They tore it down in 1982."

"You've been here that long?"

"I've been here six years now, and known Jake practically that long."

"Have you gone to the police about him, Kate?"

"No. Jake went to them when the boat disappeared. But there's not much they can do except ask some questions around the marina. I haven't been to them yet about Jake's going missing—as you say, he has been known to hole up for a few days at a time when he's pulled some bird."

Jake was a rather active pursuer of women, and I wondered if one of his casual romances might have had anything to do with his disappearance. In the United States, especially in Los Angeles, casual sex is taken just that way—casually. But in Asia, with its strong family ties and traditions and its almost maniacal insistence on saving face, things were a bit different. Although Jake's taste in women usually ran to leggy blondes or redheads, he might have gotten to know one of the local Chinese women a bit too well.

For many, sex is the motor that turns their wheels. In the world I live in, the world of entertainment, it is the coin of the realm. It sells designer jeans and toothpaste and beer and wine and shampoo. It fills the coffers of singles bars in Marina del Rey and New York's Third Avenue and similar venues all over the country. And it gives the guys in the locker room something to talk about besides the fourth quarter.

How many places of recreation would be empty if there was no chance of anyone getting laid? Beaches would be the province of small children with pails and shovels instead of smooth-skinned gods and goddesses working on their tans to impress one another. Monopoly and Scrabble sales would zoom, people would read more books, and the Internet chat rooms would implode into themselves.

And perhaps Jake McKay wouldn't have vanished suddenly and without a trace.

These were just a few of my conjectures as we pulled into the parking area at the foot of the hill behind the luxury apartment building where Jake and Boomer and Katherine lived on the edge of Repulse Bay. One of my other musings was why this feisty, windblown woman with the rumbly baritone and the cornflower blue eyes was attracting me so damned much when I should have been thinking about more pressing matters.

Chapter Three

Their flat was not much different than one might find in any metropolitan area, except it possessed a lovely view of the bay. It was crammed with Maori war clubs, Indian brass, and all the other random pieces of folklorica Jake had picked up in his globetrotting, including an exquisite Thai Buddha I had once made him promise to will me. At the moment, the promise didn't seem all that funny.

There was also, as Kate had said, one shelf of the bookcase devoted to the collected writings of one Anthony Holton, both hardcover and paperback editions, and even the audio-book versions. Very flattering, but then that's the kind of pal Jake was.

Missing, of course, was his framed Oscar nomination, posters from his films, and snapshots of him with various screen luminaries that almost any other actor in the world would have had hanging on his walls. Jake just didn't operate that way, and he never understood why, simply because he made his living in front of a camera, people thought he was somebody special. He was, of course, but not just because he happens to know Sean Connery personally.

If his household furnishings reflected his low-key, serendipitous personality, his choice of flat-mates certainly did not. Boomer Crane was a large, homely, hearty type in his mid-forties, and had that tire of flab around his middle so common to the autumnal years of big, athletic men. His handshake was a crusher, designed to remind that he once had been first-string fullback for the University of Arkansas Razorbacks until a hip injury had aborted his pro football aspirations. But I'd been ready for it, and gave him back almost as good as I got.

Having won his respect, he banged me heavily on the back, rearranging most of my internal organs, and told me how glad he was to meet any friend of old Jake's and how much he'd heard about me, and then he offered me a drink.

"It's three o'clock in the morning," I protested. "Don't you people ever sleep?"

"Hell, no, I stay up all night," he said, and went into the kitchen to pour the drinks.

"Well, I don't," said Katherine, "and I'm sinking slowly into the west. If you'll excuse me?"

I stood to take her outstretched hand. "Thank you for picking me up."

"Thank you for coming. If there's any way I can help, don't hesitate to ask."

"I won't," I assured her. She called her goodnight to Boomer as she disappeared down the hallway. I wondered if she was going to brush that fabulous windblown hair the prescribed one hundred strokes before she went to bed. And then Boomer was standing over me with a glass of Scotch, served British-fashion with no ice. I was delighted to discover, upon sipping, that it was Dalwhinnie Single Malt. I found out later that it was Jake's liquor.

"We really appreciate your coming, Kate and me," he said. "This is a sad fucking thing to happen to a man like Jake McKay."

"You and he are pretty close, I guess."

He squinched up his face. "Well now, that's the funny thing—we aren't. I mean, we're friends and all, but we don't really buddy around too much together."

"Why is that?"

"We're both too busy chasing birds," he said with a leer, and I could readily understand why Jake didn't spend his leisure hours in the company of Boomer Crane. He was everything Jake was not. I wondered how many football awards and plaques and photos of himself stiff-arming real or imaginary linebackers Boomer had on the walls of his room. Or how many fold-outs of the Playmate of the Month.

"The other thing is, I travel a lot. Half the time I'm off the island. So I don't know Jake's habits or his friends real well."

"How *is* the export business?"

He slurped his drink. "It keeps food on the table and keeps me out of trouble. And they're real understanding when I want to take a few months off."

"You do that often?"

He nodded. "Anytime there's someplace I can make me some real bread. Rwanda last year. Before that, Bangladesh, Laos, and so many places in Africa I can't recall them. Of course, those boogies are always changing the names of their countries at every whip-stitch."

Boogies, was it? I was beginning to dislike Boomer Crane rather vigorously.

"How do you make money there?" I asked, although from the places he'd named I already knew.

His chest swelled with pride. "I'm a soldier of fortune," he said.

"You mean you're a mercenary?"

He frowned. "That's kind of an old-fashioned word. We don't like it much—it's got a negative connotation."

"Sorry," I lied.

"See, I got this hip problem, come from a crackback block by an Ole Miss tackle. Besides which, I was too young for 'Nam. And I'm just naturally combatative."

Combatative? Apparently he'd gotten through his English courses at Arkansas with the gentleman's C they award varsity athletes.

"That's why I love football," he went on. "You learn survival, you learn second effort, and you learn how to win. Football or mortar shells, it's the same principle."

He leaned forward, hands on his thighs, warming to his subject. "Life-and-death situations, yeah. That's what turns me on and keeps me going. Africa, Asia, the Middle East, South America—in most of the rest of the world death is more accepted than back in the states." He chuckled. "There's an old rattletrap train that goes from Bangkok to Singapore and back—I've ridden it maybe thirty times. The guerrillas up in the hills snipe at it as it goes by, and everyone just casually lies down on the floor until the shooting stops. There aren't any windows in the train anymore because the guerrillas kept shooting them out. Now the railroad figures it's just cheaper to hang white curtains instead of glass. It's just a way of life."

"A way of death, it sounds like."

"Only if you don't do it right." He sat up. "I can snap a man's neck with one arm. I can cover a hundred yards in twelve seconds flat and you'll never hear a footstep. I know just the right place to stick in a bayonet so's it goes in all the way without hitting any bones. I'm good. Damned good. And I get top dollar whenever I go."

"Does the question of right and wrong ever enter in?"

"Hell, I'd fight my grandma if the price was right." He took another slobber of his drink and looked at me carefully; I've never learned the fine art of not letting my feelings show on my face.

"That makes you sick, doesn't it? Well, look, everybody does what they've got to do. I personally think sitting around looking at other people doing their lives and then writing about it is a pussy way to make a living," he said without rancor. "Besides, all writers are fairies."

I laughed. It was either that or take a swing at him, and after what he'd just told me that seemed like a bad idea.

"At least you got a sense of humor," he said. "But I accept you, and I drink with you. Hell, I even like you."

"Then why are you baiting me?"

He grinned. "It's just my way. To see if you can take it."

"Then you are judging me."

His eyes were shiny. "You're a pretty bright guy, Tony."

"Anthony," I corrected him. "It's a pussy name, but I like it."

We were silent for a bit. Outside the pink and gold streaks of morning were beginning to dapple the sky. Finally I asked, "Why the autobiography? You didn't have to tell me all that."

"You'd have asked eventually. That's what you're here for, to ask questions. I figured we could save a lot of mealy-mouthing around if I told you up front."

"You're pretty bright too, Boomer, once you knock off the good-ol'-boy shit."

He put down his drink. "Damn straight I am. And I'll tell you this: Jake McKay was a highly visible resident here, because of his movies. It's a big city, but there's only around fifty thousand Caucasians, mostly Brits, and we all hang out in the same seven or eight gin mills. So that makes it a very small town for a guy like Jake, whose kisser shows up on the Late Movie every week and who has dinner with visiting movie stars and cats around a lot and spends a lot of money."

"Agreed. But what's your point?"

"My point is, if I was hustling three-card monte, if I wanted financial backing to make perfume out of pig shit, if I was running any kind of a game or scam, Jake McKay would be the first guy in town I'd call up and invite to lunch."

"Are you?" I said. "Running a game?"

"All sorts of 'em. But not on Jake. You don't fuck your friends."

This from a man who'd fight his own grandmother for the right price.

He expanded, nodding his head in the direction of Kate's room. "That's why that little gal in there can live in the same flat with two randy old goats like Jake and me and not have a lock on her door."

"An old-fashioned Southern gentleman."

"You damn straight. Cheers." He drained the glass. "Gotta go take care of this cottonmouth," he said, waving the empty glass. "Can I top yours off?"

I shook my head and he went into the kitchen. I don't know how he was able to drink that way in the wee hours of the morning without passing out cold.

"I hear you and Jake were shipmates in some sort of big yacht race," I called loud enough for him to hear me in the kitchen.

"The annual South China Sea Race," he hollered back, "but it's nothing all that formal." He came back into the living room and resumed his seat. "The boats are all privately owned by rich guys, a couple of them Chinese but mostly Brits and Aussies. It's the rich man's cure for island fever, I suppose, and we get a lot of that here in HK. Anyhow—there are various classes of competition, depending on your boat. But don't get the idea it's just Sunday sailors. The South China Sea can get pretty nasty. Boats break up, masts snap in the wind. To my knowledge we've never lost anyone, but . . ."

"How long does the race take?"

"Anywhere from four to ten days, depending on wind and weather and how good your boat is and how good you are. We leave from the Aberdeen Yacht Club and sail across and around Corregidor and into Manila Bay, and at the end, when the last boat is in, there's a giant piss-up where everybody drinks and fucks and gets rowdy. That's the reason for the whole damn race in the first place."

"No prize money?"

"Except for Jake and me, these guys are big-rich, Holton. They don't need the money, they need the bragging rights. And that lasts for about two or three weeks and then everyone forgets about it until the next year. Strictly for giggles."

"And for getting your rocks off on the whole man-against-the-sea kind of thing," I observed.

He looked at me strangely. "Something like that."

"I hear you came in second this year. Who won?"

"A very rich Chinese named Jimmy Yee. Owns the biggest textile plant in Hong Kong. He also owns restaurants in Tsim Sha Tsui, some apartment blocks in Kowloon, a television production company—which is how Jake knows him—and I don't know what else. Young guy, around thirty-five or so, his mother was an *amah* and he started out with spit about eight years ago."

That Jimmy Yee could have made such a fortune from humble beginnings was impressive—if he was legitimate. It didn't seem to connect to anything about Jake's disappearance, but I filed it away anyhow. "No prize money, but lots of private bets, I imagine?"

"Sure, that's part of the fun," Boomer said.

"Jake?"

"Sure."

"Big money?"

"That's a relative thing. He had a few bets going, not much more than a couple thousand each. The biggest one was with a couple of guys named Lloyd Sturdevant and Duncan McLoughlin. They have a nice boat called *The Daisy Dell*. Sturdevant wanted to put it up against *The Lady* but Jake wouldn't go for it. He'd been trying to buy Jake's boat for about a year—but Jake would sooner sell his first-born child, if he had one."

"Tell me more about Sturdevant and McLoughlin."

Boomer shrugged and waved a hand in the air as if the two men were not important enough to discuss. "Sturdevant's American. I don't know how he made his money, but he's got a shit-pot full of it, and invested it in real estate here. McLoughlin's a Brit, from the north of England. He talks like Paul McCartney. He's a real mean sumbitch, as opposed to Sturdevant, who's quite the charmer. But they both turn everything they touch into gold."

"You think they'd be bad enough sports to steal the boat that beat them?"

"They don't have to steal, Holton, they're rich."

"Yes, but you said Jake wouldn't sell."

He looked at me levelly, seriously. "You think they have something to do with Jake going missing? That's a hell of a long shot."

"I've spent my life betting long shots. Is there anyone in town Jake just plain doesn't get along with? Any enemies? Even minor ones?"

Boomer hunched his big shoulders and thought it over. "Jake might have put his dick somewhere he shouldn't—that happens to the best of us. But nobody really dislikes him that I know of."

I took a deep breath, but it didn't relieve the pressure that was building up inside my throat, and the feeling of unease. I held out my glass to him. "I've changed my mind about that drink," I said.

★ ★ ★ ★ ★

They let me sleep until ten-thirty, and when Kate knocked on the door to wake me, I knew I hadn't slept long enough. I never sparkle in the morning, even at my best, and after a long trip and the drinking marathon the night before I was far from my best now.

"I thought we'd go across to the Peninsula Hotel for Sunday brunch," she said from the doorway, kindly pretending to ignore the fact that I was naked beneath the sheet, my hair was completely askew, and I looked like hell. "If you've never had their orange pancakes you're in for one of the great treats. I remember Jake saying you were something of a gourmet."

I rubbed my hand over my face and combed my hair with splayed fingers. "I didn't come here to do tourist stuff, Kate."

"It's worth your time," she assured me. "Everyone who's anyone goes to the Pen for Sunday brunch. To be seen as much as for the food. You'll get to shake hands with some of the people you'll want to talk to later, and it will be that much easier for you if they've met you socially first."

"As long as I don't have to wear a tie," I said.

The drive northward over the peak was beautiful, the scenery almost hurtful in the crisp clarity of mid-morning light, and I was better able to see Kate than I had been in the darkness of the previous evening. She had chosen a dark brown silk dress that accented her blondish hair, which still looked windblown.

The Star Ferry is a Hong Kong legend, playing the waters of Victoria Harbour between the island and the Kowloon side, providing commuters with a view that was exciting and awe-inspiring, both during the day when the green of the peak rose above the towering skyscrapers of the

Central District, and at night, when the vista of advertising neon looked like a diorama in some sort of Disney Tomorrowland, sprawling beyond the limits of peripheral vision and lighting up the entire sky. Kate told me the signs were not allowed to utilize moving or chasing lights because of the proximity of the airport, since they didn't want pilots becoming confused and landing their 747s on Nathan Road.

But this was a warm, sunny morning, and I wanted to stand out on the bow and suck up the view. Kate was a good sport about it, standing there with me with the wind tossing her hair and blowing her dress provocatively against lissome legs.

The Star Ferry terminal on the Kowloon side was two short blocks from the Peninsula, and we strolled down Salisbury Road past the Space Museum to the hotel that symbolized to many the very essence of the British Empire, along with Raffles in Singapore and London's Savoy.

Brunch was served at one end of the long, ornate lobby, and though there was a respectable representation of Europeans scattered among the beautifully set tables, most of the diners were Chinese. There is something about the Chinese language that makes speaking it at the top of one's voice almost imperative; to most untrained ears it sounds like violent arguments. There are many dialects in China, most unintelligible to each other, such as Hakka, Shanghainese, Cantonese, which was the language most spoken in Hong Kong, and the official dialect of the People's Republic, Mandarin. They all sounded equally baffling to me.

But there was something in the look of these well-groomed, mostly elderly and almost exclusively male Chinese at the Pen that made me think they spoke not only their language and mine, but several others as well, including the ones understood all over the planet—power and money.

Kate was pointing out some of the more interesting of our co-diners, her running commentary like that of a tour guide on a bus tour of movie star homes in Beverly Hills. "That's Lee Ming," she was saying. "Investment banker. Hardly any big money changes hands in Asia without his fingerprints on it. Over there is Cheung Ho—executive vice president of Honkers and Shankers." I'm sure I looked blank, because she hastened to translate. "The Hong Kong and Shanghai Bank. And that young one over there, that's Jimmy Yee."

"Where," I said, almost throwing my neck out to turn and look.

"Don't be obvious," she admonished, "it's considered rude. Over there near the corner."

I looked again, this time more discreetly, but the slim, boyish man in the Armani suit with a pretty young Chinese woman opposite him, had caught me rubbernecking and inclined his head toward me ever so slightly, royalty acknowledging the peasants along the carriage route.

"That's the hotshot sailor, hmm?"

She smiled. "I see you didn't waste your time talking to Boomer. Yes, that's the man who came in first in the yacht race."

"Do you know him personally?" When she nodded, I said, "Introduce me."

"Why?"

"I like winners," I said. "Maybe some of it will rub off."

"After breakfast, then." She poured tea from an exquisite porcelain pot and toasted me with her cup. "To winners," she said, and I was more than happy to drink to that.

With all the noise in the lobby I didn't really hear the commotion; I sensed it behind me. Turning, I saw an enormous black man raising total hell with the headwaiter, and doing so at full volume. He was easily four and a half feet around at the waist, and the expensive tailoring of his slacks and his white linen jacket couldn't disguise the layers of fat that puddled over each other like melting ice cream.

The handsome Mediterranean-looking woman at his side did not bother to hide the fact she was embarrassed at the fuss her companion was making. Apparently he was unhappy with the table he'd been given, although it was obvious it was the only one currently vacant. That didn't deter him from his bullish abuse of the Chinese headwaiter, and finally most of the people at the tables had turned to look at him. There was disdain, and much disapproval, but mostly I saw outright hatred in their eyes. In America I might have attributed it to his blackness, but here in Hong Kong I believe it was because no one who was not Chinese was perceived to have a right to be so obnoxious.

To the maitre d's credit, he never let go of his dignity, never fawned or cowered, and never backed down; instead he was almost detached, like a man standing across the room observing the disturbance. There was none of the loss of face by which Asians set such store. On the contrary, it was the fat man who was losing the face—and the argument as well. Finally he plopped gracelessly into the chair he'd been offered and murmured dire imprecations at the headwaiter, who held the other chair for the lady with all the grace and aplomb of a man who had just come out on top.

"I did mention that Averell Brown was a bit hard to take, didn't I?"

I was taken aback. "That's Averell Brown?" Not only was his name unfamiliar to me, but his face as well, and with all my film contacts in Hollywood I was sure I'd have either run into him somewhere or at least have heard of him. There are few of Brown's race producing films in Los Angeles, and so the ones who do tend to be very visible. I wondered what kind of game he was running here in China.

"Introduce me to him too, Kate."

She groaned softly. "I was hoping to sneak out without having to talk to him. He's really the most unpleasant man. I was pretending not to notice him."

"That's like not noticing Mount McKinley. I want to meet him."

"Not while I'm eating," Kate said.

As promised, the pancakes were superb. Uniquely delicate, with the subtlety of flavor only the great Asian chefs seem to master. As good as they were, though, I kept being distracted glancing at Averell Brown and Jimmy Yee. My interest in my stunning companion had not lessened one whit, either. All in all, it was a memorable brunch.

After we finished eating, we headed for Jimmy Yee's table. He rose as we approached. He was short, much shorter than either Kate or I and I tried to scrunch down a little so he would suffer no perceived loss of face. He sported a Fu Manchu–type mustache and goatee, but when he spoke it was in the soft, cultured tones of a James Mason or Alec Guinness.

"Jimmy," Kate said, "may I present Mr. Anthony Holton, from the U.S. He's a good friend of Jake McKay's."

We shook hands and he inclined his head slightly. I couldn't help noticing Kate had called him by his first name while referring to me as "mister," and I wondered if there was a none-too-subtle racism at work there, a lack of respect that was perhaps a vestigial remnant of British colonialism. Considering that most of the money floating around Hong Kong was Jimmy Yee's, I found Kate's attitude curious and upsetting.

"I am honored to meet you, Mr. Yee," I said. He noticed the pointed respect and a little jolt of psychic energy passed between us. He was rather handsome, especially when he smiled. The impression of royalty I'd gotten from him from across the room was not entirely dispelled up close, but it was tempered by a certain likable softness.

"Will you join me for tea, Mr. Holton?" he asked, and then added, "and Miss Longley?"

Kate looked at me entreatingly. She obviously didn't want to have tea with him. She was my strongest ally in town, and I didn't want to place her in an uncomfortable position. But I made a note to ask her later what was going on.

"We must decline, Mr. Yee, with thanks. But I'd be most interested in speaking with you at another, more mutually convenient time."

His sparse eyebrows lifted. "Oh? Perhaps later this afternoon, then. I will be on my boat." His smile widened. "And at that time I shall offer you something more potent than tea."

"I'm anxious to see your boat, sir. I've heard many good things about her."

"I am pleased by that. Half past four, then?"

We shook hands again and Kate and I took our leave. As we crossed the lobby she refused to make eye contact with me, and her chin was jutting out at that stubborn angle I was coming to recognize even after such short acquaintance.

"I assume you know where his boat is?" I said, and she nodded grimly.

We were aiming at Averell Brown's table, and as we approached I was able to get a better look at the man. He was bearded, and the fullness of his beard added to the width of his chubby face. He was shoveling breakfast into his mouth at a rapid rate, too busy eating to relate to the woman with him, and she was turned slightly away from him as she ate, as if to convey with body language that she was seated with this man by some gross and egregious act of negligence on the part of the management.

Brown looked up and waved us into chairs before we could say anything. "Hello, Kate," he said. "And Anthony Holton, isn't it? Recognized you from your book jackets. It was Jake McKay first turned me onto your work." I could see the half-chewed pancakes in his mouth as he spoke. "My wife, Rosa." Rosa Brown nodded uneasily, as though by acknowledging her own presence here she was making a shameful admission. I don't know, maybe she was.

Brown didn't offer a handshake, and it wasn't because he was too busy eating. It annoyed me. It was also insulting, and I'm sure Brown knew it. The belligerence fairly bristled from him, but I didn't take it personally. I suppose he had little use for the white race, and I was irked that we couldn't approach each other as just people.

In hindsight, I believe Averell Brown was a man who'd had to fight and rend and tear and cheat for everything he had, and naturally assumed that everyone else wanted to strip him of it. His blackness simply gave him a platform on which to plant his feet, but I'm sure he was just as bellicose and rude with everyone, regardless of race, color, creed, or national origin. Brown was an Equal Opportunity Asshole.

But I sensed there was more to him than simply being uncouth. Perhaps it was his sheer chutzpah—throwing his considerable weight around in such a high-handed manner—that led me to believe that here was a man intrinsically dangerous, who stood ready to unlock the cage that held in his subcutaneous violence. What made him all the more frightening is that I didn't know what form his rage might take. A physical attack from one so morbidly obese was unlikely and not fearsome; yet somewhere there were resources, wellsprings from which he drew his strength and arrogance, and I thought it might be interesting sometime, albeit hazardous, to discover them.

"What brings you to Hong Kong?" he said between bites.

"I'm visiting Jake," I said. If he had any reaction to that, he managed to conceal it completely.

"Jake. I love him. One of my best friends."

"I hear he's doing a picture for you."

Suspicion sprouted all over him like the hackles on an angered watchdog. "We've already got a working screenplay, so there's nothing in the project for you," he said. "We're going after only name stars. Tom Cruise. Bobby DeNiro. Denzel." That last was undoubtedly a reference to actor Denzel Washington, though I doubted Brown knew him well enough to call him by his first name, nor did he refer to Robert DeNiro as "Bobby" to his face.

"Nic Cage"—another diminutive—"is dying to do it, but he's committed to another project." He jabbed a finger into my chest, and it kind of hurt. "It's a great fucking script."

I told him I was sure it was.

"Action pictures sell, man. They eat that shit up in the international market. I should know—I produced *Kona Coast* and it was a fucking blockbuster!"

I glanced at Kate, who wasn't cinema-wise enough to know that *Kona Coast* was no blockbuster, enjoying marginal success at best, and that a man named Stan Keppelman had produced it. I happened to know that because Keppelman and I used to play tennis together. Mrs. Brown either didn't hear the bald-faced lie, or she'd heard it so often in the past she no longer cared.

"This one's gonna be even bigger," Brown said. "Especially if we can get Tom Cruise."

"Jake sure is lucky to be in on a prestigious project like this," I said dryly, but Brown was too busy eating to catch the sarcasm. I knew the Chinese were among the world's most dedicated gamblers, and I wondered if anyone in town would be crazy enough to take my wager that Tom Cruise and "Bobby" DeNiro never heard of Averell Brown, that the film would never be made, and that Brown would leave Hong Kong with a lot of somebody else's money in his pocket.

"Have you spent much time with Jake lately?" I asked.

"Sure," Brown said, his voice thickening. "When he's not too busy with his fancy stateside friends. When he's not having dinner with fucking Gene Hackman and doesn't invite me. When he thinks about the last time anyone offered him a decent part in a major feature, or when he needs a dinner or a car or a piece of Chinese ass."

I bit back my annoyance. "When did you see him last?"

The suspicious pig eyes almost disappeared behind the fat moons of his cheeks. "You ask a lotta fucking questions, Holton. Why do you want to know?"

Kate didn't seem to be flashing me any warning signs, so I went ahead and told Brown about Jake and his boat disappearing.

He leaned his ponderous bulk over the table at me. "You saying I done it?" he said, spraying me with food.

"Of course not. Just trying to get a line on what might

41

have happened, and I thought you could help, seeing as how you're Jake's best friend."

"Shit!" he exploded, throwing his napkin down on his plate and sending an explosion of powdered sugar into the atmosphere and all over his jacket like an attack of instant dandruff. "I was counting on him for the picture! Motherfucker!"

"Your concern for Jake is touching," I said, "but I'm here in Hong Kong to find him, and I'm talking to you because you and Jake seem to be involved in a project for some peculiar reason."

"What you mean, peculiar reason?" he said. The more agitated he became, the more his speech took on the flavor of Harlem.

"I think you're as phony as a drag queen in a ladies' room, for one thing," I said. "You didn't produce *Kona Coast* because I happen to know who did. You can shuck and jive these Chinese people you're trying to hustle, but don't pull it on me. I lived and worked in the industry for years in Los Angeles, and I never heard of you."

He became livid, firing off more scraps of his meal from between his lips as he shouted. "You come on home with me, I'll show you a picture of me and Bruce Willis."

"I can show you a picture of me with Bill Clinton," I said, "but that doesn't make me the First Lady."

The more livid he became, the more scraps of his brunch flew from his mouth. "You're gonna be talking out of the other side of your mouth if I send a couple of my Black Muslim friends around to teach you some manners."

I wiped the pancakes off my face and stood up. "When they come," I said, "make sure they come up with a more believable story. You can bore me, you can spit your breakfast at me, but don't try to insult my intelligence."

With a nod to Mrs. Brown, who had watched the entire scene without emotion as though it were TV footage of a forest fire in a distant state, I walked toward the far end of the lobby where the street door glowed with midmorning light, Kate hurriedly following in my wake. I felt every eye in the place burning holes in my back as if a little kid were working on it with sunlight and a magnifying glass. It was my biggest and most attentive live audience since my days apprenticing in a summer theatre in Litchfield, Connecticut.

Chapter Four

I waited on the sidewalk in front of the Peninsula until finally Kate came out to join me, somewhat unnerved and looking very disapproving.

"I behaved badly," I said, and that's the closest anyone will ever come to hearing an Anthony Holton apology. I don't believe in them, because they never do any good anyway, and because I've never cared for the taste or texture of crow.

"No worse than he," Kate said. "And the Chinese in there have probably chalked you up as one more ugly American and will forget about it before their tea can cool. I just loathe scenes, that's all. I'd walk a mile to avoid them."

We began strolling back toward the Star Ferry, the breeze blowing off the water refreshing in the mid-afternoon heat.

"Is Brown really a liar and a phony?"

"That's how I read him," I said. "I think his game plan is to get the most money from whatever rich Chinese will buy his snake oil, and then get out of town before they realize he's skinned them and put some finely-shaved bamboo splinters into his Kung Pao chicken."

"You think Jake was on to him?"

"Sure, Jake's no dummy. But I suppose he was playing him along just on the off chance that Brown's movie *did* get made. Maybe Brown knew Jake had him pegged and wanted him out of the way before he blew the whistle."

I had taken her elbow with my hand, and when I said that a little shudder ran through her body. I put my arm around her waist and was pleased at the easy way she leaned into me, accepting the familiarity.

We got to the Hong Kong Hotel near the Ocean Terminal and without consulting each other we veered off to cross the lobby and settle into a booth in the bamboo-and-hanging-plant bar opposite the main desk. The subdued lighting flattered her, but then I'd yet to see her in a light that didn't. I ordered a Kir for her and a Glenfiddich on the rocks for me.

"Do you always come after people as hard as you did Averell Brown?" she said.

"That's how you learn things," I said. "When you pressure people they say and do things they might not ordinarily do when they're all loosey-goosey."

"You Americans!" she said, laughing. "Loosey-goosey!"

I laughed with her and then leaned forward and put my hand over hers to ensure that I had her attention.

"Kate—why didn't you want to sit down at Jimmy Yee's table?"

She frowned and looked away. "It may be hard for a Yank to understand, but we have a fairly rigid social structure here. We Europeans do business with the Chinese, but we don't much socialize. It isn't done."

That wasn't entirely true, but I supposed it wasn't entirely false, either. I knew from previous trips that Caucasian men who dated Chinese women were socially beyond the pale in Hong Kong, and that fooling around with a local lady might result in her appearing at your hotel room door the next morning with her parents, cousins, grandmothers, and all their worldly possessions, wondering when they were all coming back to America with you.

"Are you being straight with me, Kate?"

"What is straight?" she snapped, shaking her head in the manner of someone who's just bumped it hard. "This is Hong Kong. Things are different here."

She waited for me to speak, but I didn't. I knew she'd evaded my question and I wasn't about to let her off the hook. I just looked at her.

Finally: "I don't particularly like the Chinese, all right?"

"Then you've picked a peculiar place to live."

"We don't always pick—oh, hell!" She took a bird-like sip of her Kir. "All right, then, if you must know. I was deeply involved with someone here for the past two years, and he's just recently left me and taken up with a Chinese girl, and I don't particularly want to be around them and be nice to them right now, that's all."

"You can't blame two billion people because you're mad at one of them," I said. "By your logic, I should be angry with you about the Boston Massacre."

"It's not the same at all," she said, making "at all" one word with a harsh, dentalized "T."

"Maybe not," I said. "Can we talk about something else, then?"

She rolled her eyes heavenward. "God, that would be wonderful!"

"Jake's boat boy."

"Johnson Lau?"

"Does he speak English well enough for me to ask him some questions?"

"Johnson was educated in the U.S. He speaks English better than you do. He's usually at the Yacht Club—where Jimmy Yee berths his boat. Perhaps you can kill two birds with one stone this afternoon. However, I think I'll pass, if you don't mind. Can you make it around on your own?"

"I think so. I can even have dinner on my own—but I'd rather not. Will you join me later?"

"That can be arranged," she said. "We'll do something

46

really touristy—one of the floating restaurants in Aberdeen."

"Sounds like fun," I lied.

"Good. Meet me at the Sea Palace at half past seven, then. I'll phone ahead for a table."

We took the ferry back to the Hong Kong side. Kate picked up her car and disappeared and I decided to kill an hour having a drink at the Conrad International Hotel. I walked into the ornate lobby and headed for the bar. When I'm in Bangkok it practically takes a papal decree to get me into a bar alone, but being away from my own turf was different. Besides, I wanted to digest the morning's happenings in the quiet of a cool cocktail lounge where there were no sad drunks, weekend bachelors on the prowl, or Hawaiian-shirted tourists talking too loud.

But I quickly changed my mind about solitude because I ran into an old friend. The upside of being an old expatriate bum like me is that almost everywhere you go, you run into someone you know.

Jackie Ho was assistant guest relations director of the hotel, and during my previous stays I had quickly learned that if I wanted anything done efficiently, she was the one to ask about it. She was in her mid-twenties, slim and doe-like in her standard-issue dark blue suit. Her eyes were big and shiny and alert, and they danced when she smiled. She didn't cover the smile with her hand as many Asian women did, either. She'd been educated in England so that her enunciation was near perfect, and the curious sing-song cadence of Cantonese only occasionally colored her speech.

"Anthony Holton," she beamed. In America I would have hugged her in greeting, but this was Asia and she was a hotel employee, so I simply extended my hand to hers, which was long and tapered and felt cool to the touch. I invited her to join me for a drink.

When we were installed in a corner booth in the dark, cool bar, I asked her whether she'd seen Jake McKay recently.

"Not for about a week," she said. "I understand he's very busy now, because he's getting ready to be in Mr. Brown's new movie."

"You know Mr. Brown?"

"Everyone in Hong Kong knows Mr. Brown," she said. "He comes here a lot, too. He's hard to miss." She ducked her head slightly, the good employee not wanting to say anything derogatory about a customer.

"You don't miss much of what goes on around here, do you, Jackie?"

"Well, sitting in the middle of the lobby the way I do . . ."

"I imagine you know about everything that goes on in Hong Kong," I said. "Do you know where Mr. Brown is getting the money to produce his movie?"

"I don't know. He's had lunches and dinners with many wealthy gentlemen of the island right here in Nicholini's. As a matter of fact, the last time I saw Mr. McKay he was dining with Mr. Brown and Mr. Jimmy Yee. One day last week."

I listened to the hum of the air conditioning and the drone of the piped-in Muzak. "Did you know that someone stole Jake McKay's boat, Jackie? And that he's been missing for several days?"

Her eyes widened in real surprise. "Oh no!" she said. "Poor Jake."

"That's why I'm here. To help him. Can you think of anyone I might talk to?"

She thought about it for a minute. "You've spoken to his flat-mate, Mr. Crane?"

I nodded.

"And the lady, too?"

"Yes."

She frowned. "Well, Jake has a lot of friends. You might speak to Mr. Stanley Nivens," she suggested. "They were close."

"Where can I find him?"

"He's a journalist, I believe, and he's frequently at the Foreign Correspondent's Club. And he's usually at the Godown on Sunday nights—it's a little bar in the Central District—about three blocks from here. You know it?"

"I know it," I said. The Godown was a favorite of non-Asian expatriates, and Jake had taken me there often. "Do you know if there was any particular lady Jake was seeing?"

"There were lots of different ladies, like always. Most of them were flight attendants—they all usually stay out in Causeway Bay." She looked sad. "I'm sure Jake is all right, Anthony. I hope so. He's always been one of my favorite people."

We chatted a bit longer, mostly the mindless trivia old acquaintances exchange while trying to reconnect. Then I said, "And how have you been, Jackie? How's your husband and your baby?"

For a brief moment a look of unbearable sadness crossed her face, and then she camouflaged it. "My husband and son are living in Manila, now," she said too brightly. "We're—separated."

That was a surprise; divorce among the Chinese was as rare as a bronc rider at the premiere of *Rigoletto*, and I wondered what sort of apocalypse had divided the House of Ho. I wasn't going to ask, though; curiosity had caused the death of more than one cat.

She told me she had to get back to her desk so we said

our good-byes, and I promised to come and have lunch with her one day next week. Then I went to the main entrance of the hotel and had the Pakistani doorman hail me a taxi.

I headed back over the Peak, and the sunset gave the panorama of Repulse Bay still another dimension. In Los Angeles a cab ride of that length might have cost a day's pay, but here in Hong Kong it was less than ten dollars, and the driver was thrilled to pieces when I tipped him an additional ten.

At the Aberdeen Yacht Club, a few miles west of Repulse Bay itself, I sought out the club steward and was told I could find Johnson Lau working on one of the luxurious cabin cruisers moored at the dock. I took off my jacket, because the setting sun was still warm, and followed his directions past several million dollars' worth of nautical hardware to the end of the pier where the giant powerboat was moored.

Johnson Lau was tall for a Chinese, and as ruggedly handsome as any movie star. His zest for life showed in his quick, open smile and his dancing eyes, and his longish hair was carefully styled and blow-dried. He was very glad to see me when I told him I was a friend of Jake's, and I was pleased to note that he used Jake's first name instead of the more formal "mister."

We walked along the jetty and talked, and the more time we spent together the more I liked Johnson Lau. He was a very charming young man.

"I feel responsible for *The Lady*," he said. "I'm the boat boy, it's my job to look after her. But the night she was stolen, I wasn't here; I was spending the night in town." He smiled sheepishly. "With a friend. When I came to work the next morning, she was gone."

I shook my head. "You don't just hide a boat the size of *The Hong Kong Lady*."

"Evidently somebody has," he said.

"The question is, where? If you were going to hide a boat around here, where would you do it?"

"There are more than two hundred islands off the coast of Hong Kong, Mr. Holton. Lantau, Cheng Chau, Lamma—those are the big ones, and there are villages there, even some hotels. Some of the smaller ones are farther away, and almost completely deserted. There are bays and inlets on most of them, plenty big enough to moor *The Lady* out of sight. It would take a month to check them all out, and you still wouldn't be sure."

"How long would it take to get to the farthest island?"

"Under sail, half a day. Or half a night, as the case was. With a powerboat, around two hours. Of course, when you're talking about the South China Sea the weather is always a factor."

I gestured at all the luxury yachts in the anchorage, which looked like the boat basin at Marina del Rey. "Any of these boats been out of here in the last few days? Say, since Thursday?"

"You're kidding," he said. "They go in and out every weekend."

"What about before the weekend? On Thursday, or Friday morning."

"Quite a few. I really only pay attention to my own boats."

"Did Mr. Jimmy Yee take his boat out, do you recall?"

"Sure. I think it was Thursday evening. He took a bunch of business types in suits for a cruise."

"How long was he gone?"

"He left just before sunset. I don't know what time he got back because I had a date that night. The boat was in its slip Friday morning."

"Was that unusual, Mr. Yee taking a night cruise?"

"Mr. Yee is like a kid with a toy about that boat. He sails her every chance he gets." He cleared his throat. "I don't mean to be rude, Mr. Holton, but could you tell me why you're asking all these questions?"

Every once in a while you have to take a chance, I suppose. We all suffer from a certain amount of paranoia; we've forgotten how to trust. I decided to trust Johnson Lau.

"Jake has been missing since Thursday, Johnson. No one has seen or heard from him. I think it might have something to do with his boat being stolen. That's why I'm here in Hong Kong. And I'm hoping you can help me."

"Missing?" Johnson looked genuinely concerned. "I don't like the sound of that."

"Neither do I."

"Jake McKay is my friend," he said. "I'd do anything for him. So you just let me know how I can help."

"I will," I said. "Maybe sooner than you think. In the meantime, I have an appointment to see Jimmy Yee. Which is his boat?"

Johnson pointed to a magnificent yacht not too far from the boathouse. It was the second largest yacht in the basin. "Mr. Yee's got company right now, though," he said. Like Jackie Ho, Johnson didn't miss much.

"Female company?"

"No."

"Then let's not worry about it."

He smiled. "You can usually reach me here at the club. If not, I'm in the phone book. Tang Lung Street in Causeway Bay. L-A-U."

"I'm staying at Jake's flat if you should hear anything. By the way, what do you think of Boomer Crane?"

"Hell of a sailor," he said.

"And?"

His smile turned inscrutable. "Hell of a sailor."

I nodded. "I really appreciate your help, Johnson." I took out a roll of bills and started to peel one off, but he held up his hand.

"You don't know the Chinese way," he said, "or I would consider that an insult. I've said that Jake was my friend."

"I apologize," I said formally, the words sounding strange on my tongue. "No insult was intended. Just the opposite." I bowed slightly and he bowed back and then we both relaxed again. "Let's touch base tomorrow."

"Good luck," he said, and we shook hands warmly. Then I turned and headed down the jetty toward Jimmy Yee's yacht.

A heavy-set and thoroughly muscled Chinese with a shaved head, wearing work clothes, was stationed at the top of the gangway, showing no inclination toward allowing me to board. I told him I was expected, and pronounced my name very carefully for him. He nodded and then turned and went into the cabin, only to reappear thirty seconds later and motion me aboard with an almost imperceptible movement of his chin. I didn't think he was employed because of his way with boat motors or his skill with an abacus. His eyes never left me as I walked up the gangway and through the open hatch into the cabin.

Jimmy Yee was dressed in sailor's whites, sipping what looked like a frozen daiquiri. He rose when I entered the cabin, as did his two visitors, both Caucasians. "Mr. Holton," Yee said, "I am pleased you could come. May I present my friends, Mr. Sturdevant and Mr. McLoughlin?"

I turned and nodded at the other two men. No one seemed inclined to shake hands. Sturdevant was the taller of the two, almost as tall as I, with a thatch of sun-blond hair and piercing blue eyes and the trim, lean body of a life-long athlete, even though he was well into his fifties. His smile was friendly enough, although I think he was so rich that he smiled all the time anyway. He wore a pullover gray cashmere sweater with no shirt under it, a pair of white duck trousers, and deck shoes. No socks. He was very strik-ing-looking, and I had the feeling he knew it.

McLoughlin was his polar opposite, short and squat with the face of a toy pug, and powerful arms and shoulders that looked ready to burst through his bright red windbreaker. He was not smiling, and the heavy down-turning lines at the corners of his full mouth led me to believe that smiling was a rarity for him. I wondered what kind of bond it was that had brought the two of them together, and decided their commonality began and ended in the pocketbook.

"Holton," Sturdevant said. "You look older than your photographs."

"I am older than my photographs," I said, unsure as to why he had attacked so quickly. McLoughlin seemed to be radiating animosity too, although his was a facial type that always looked angry and sullen.

Jimmy Yee didn't seem hostile, but he wore that bland Chinese expression most Caucasians find so difficult to read, and he was looking from one to the other of us as though we were trained pit bulls he had thrown together to watch tear each other to pieces for his own personal amuse-ment.

He bowed me into a chair and offered me a frozen dai-quiri, and when I accepted he pushed a button near his chair and a white-coated Chinese steward came in silently and fixed the drink and brought it to me.

We all chatted more or less pleasantly for a bit, as I was

sure Jimmy Yee subscribed to the Chinese philosophy that it is bad manners to come directly to the point. And as his guest, it was incumbent upon me to wait for him to get around to asking me what I wanted. When he finally did it came in a rather startling form.

"You have come to Hong Kong to investigate the disappearance of your dear friend Jake McKay. Am I correct, Mr. Holton?"

I spoke carefully. "I wasn't aware that Jake's disappearance was common knowledge, Mr. Yee."

He smiled. "It is not common knowledge. I wonder, though, why you choose to discuss it with me."

"Please be assured," I said, "that I am in no way suggesting that you have any knowledge of Jake's troubles. But you do know him, have had dealings with him, and I thought perhaps you might be able to tell me something that could be of help to me." I glanced over at Sturdevant and McLoughlin. "And you too, gentlemen. I'm told you were friends with Jake as well." The enforced formality of speech was making my head ache.

McLoughlin grunted. "Bad show, Jake falling off the edge of the earth like that. Mind you, he'll show up. Off on a toot, more than likely."

I said to Yee, "Is that a shared opinion, sir?"

"There are things we cannot know, Mr. Holton. The theft of *The Hong Kong Lady*, Jake's disappearance . . . It is possible that the two incidents are—related."

"That's what I think, too. I also heard that Mr. Sturdevant and Mr. McLoughlin here wanted very much to buy *The Lady* and that Jake wouldn't sell."

"Of course we wanted it," Sturdevant said in an aggrieved tone. "It's a hell of a boat. But we didn't steal it. Where the hell do you think we'd put it if we had?"

"Whoever stole it put it somewhere. In any case, no one has seen it—or Jake."

"If you ever do find it, you'll have hell's own time catching up with it. That's a fast boat. Cleaned our clocks, I don't mind telling you," McLoughlin grumbled. "Only Jimmy finished ahead of her in the race."

"You fellows had a large bet on that race with Jake, didn't you?"

"A gentleman doesn't discuss his gambling debts."

"Mr. McLoughlin, my best friend is missing and may be dead. Under the circumstances I don't give a brown rat's ass about your gentleman's code. I ask you again, did you lose money to Jake McKay?"

McLoughlin looked at his partner, who nodded. "Twenty thousand U.S.," he said.

I licked my suddenly dry lips. "That's a hell of a lot of money."

Sturdevant snorted. "I leave more than that as a tip at dinner."

"Nevertheless," I said, "did you pay off?"

"I wrote him a check that very night in Manila. He cashed it, too, damn his eyes."

The thrust of the conversation finally got through to Duncan McLoughlin, who seemed a bit dim-witted compared with his friend. "See here!" he snarled. "I think I resent your implication, Holton."

I turned in my chair to face him squarely. "What is there to resent if you've nothing to hide?"

"The insolence . . ."

Jimmy Yee raised his hand almost imperceptibly and McLoughlin fell silent. It was a quiet show of strength that would compel anyone to sit up a little straighter. I know I did.

For a moment there was no movement, except for the gentle rocking of waves against the yacht's hull. Then Yee said, "Jake McKay has become a good friend to us since he moved to Hong Kong. We would wish to assist you in any way we can to help him. It would be in our own best interest as well."

I sensed that Yee's use of "we" was royal, and did not encompass his two companions. "Perhaps, then, you could fill me in on a few things. As you know, I made the acquaintance of a Mr. Averell Brown this morning."

McLoughlin's laugh was an ugly bark. "The town is buzzing with it. About time someone told off that bloody bastard."

I ignored him. "I've been told that Jake was to be in a film Brown is going to produce here in Hong Kong, and that it is being financed locally. Does anyone know who the angel is?"

They all looked blank.

"Sorry, that's a show business term. The investor. The person or persons financing the film."

"May I inquire," Yee said carefully, "why this information is pertinent to your inquiry?"

"I don't know if it is," I admitted. "I'm just trying to put some pieces together to see if they fit."

Yee nodded, and thought for a moment. Then he glanced over at Sturdevant. "I have the honor of being the principal investor."

Somehow that didn't surprise me. "May I inquire, sir, as to the amount of your investment in this film?"

"None of your goddamn business!" Sturdevant exploded, and it was like getting a bucket of ice water in the chest.

Yee flashed him a look of caution, and then smiled at

me, but the smile was connected to a string that could easily be pulled taut. "That question *is* impertinent, is it not?"

"I beg your pardon, Mr. Yee, but with my friend in possible danger, I'm not feeling very polite."

Jimmy Yee sat very straight in his chair, both feet on the floor, and looked at me in an unusually direct way. Finally he said, "The figure is to be seven million dollars—in United States currency."

I nodded my thanks. Seven million is a lot of money to anyone, but in Hollywood terms a very small budget picture. Certainly not the kind of vehicle that would attract a highly paid star like Tom Cruise. "You said you were the principal investor, sir. May I know the identity of the others?"

Yee bobbed his head as though he'd been caught in a slight indiscretion and was now trying to be graceful about it. "I am the only investor, for all practical purposes."

"Practical purposes?"

"I represent a syndicate of other investors."

I sucked in a breath and jumped in. The water was cold. "Are you aware that in today's filmmaking market seven million dollars wouldn't even pay the salary of someone of the stature of Tom Cruise? That a film of the size and scope suggested by Mr. Brown would cost in the neighborhood of sixty to eighty million?"

Jimmy Yee's sparse eyebrows puckered into a deep frown. "I do not understand," he said.

"From where I sit, Mr. Yee, it appears that Mr. Brown has no intention of making a film at all. The whole idea is to get your money and then run. Brown is a phony. He claims to have produced films that he had nothing to do with, at least not as the producer. He's a con man, and he's running around Hong Kong with a script trying to con you."

McLoughlin jumped to his feet angrily. "We've been bum-fucked!" he exclaimed.

We. So Sturdevant and McLoughlin were part of Yee's "syndicate." I wasn't surprised, but it was good to know for sure.

"How much have you given Brown so far, in hard cash?" I said.

Yee put his delicate hands over his eyes. "One hundred thousand dollars, in round figures. Mr. Brown referred to it, I believe, as seed money."

"That's a lot of seed."

"All right, then," Sturdevant said, "but what's all this have to do with McKay?"

"Perhaps nothing. But maybe Jake realized what Brown was up to and Brown didn't want his game spoiled."

Yee brought his face up out of his hands and stared at me icily, and too late I remembered the fate of the messenger who brought bad news to the king.

"I'm sorry to be the one to have to tell you this, Mr. Yee."

"You seem to have involved yourself rather extensively in our affairs, Mr. Holton."

"Inadvertently, I assure you. I don't care who's doing business with whom unless it somehow relates to what's happened to Jake."

"Yes," Yee said. "We would hope that you will keep what you have surmised to yourself."

"Why would I tell anyone?"

He shrugged. "Mr. Brown may not be what he seemed. It is possible the same might be said of you."

"It is possible," I admitted, "and I can't make you believe me. All I want is Jake McKay."

"Let us assume it is so. But there are others whose motives are perhaps not so pure as yours. We would prefer that what we have discussed here remains here between us."

"Of course," I said.

Face. The terrible loss of face Jimmy Yee would suffer if the local financial community learned he had been suckered by a foul-mouthed, jive-talking American who had dangled visions of international grosses and nubile and obliging Hollywood lovelies in front of his nose might be a wound from which he would never completely recover. I didn't give enough of a damn one way or the other, so it was no skin off my nose—or my face—to agree to confidentiality.

Then again, I thought of the muscular, shaven-domed Chinese on deck and wasn't sure how easily I would have walked off Jimmy Yee's boat without acquiescing.

Yee stood up, and I did, too. "You must excuse me now, Mr. Holton. I'm afraid we must make certain—arrangements—for the recovery of our money."

Little fingers of ice caressed the back of my neck as I wondered if I had not just condemned Averell Brown to death by poking my unwanted nose into his business.

I preferred to think not. I preferred to think I had simply queered Brown's scam, cost him some ill-gotten cash, and saved these three men, and Jake McKay, from having their chains jerked by a bad-mannered sharpie. Averell Brown would simply have his toys taken from him, and that was that.

That's what I preferred to think.

I walked past the tough-looking muscleman on the deck and back down toward the clubhouse, hoping to get another chance to speak with Johnson Lau, but he had already gone for the day. I strolled around the marina for a while and then took a taxi to the village of Aberdeen.

Still called Heung Kong Tsai by the Chinese, Aberdeen will boggle the mind of most Westerners. To see such a seething mass of humanity living and dying aboard their boats, often not setting foot on dry land for months or years at a time, keeping pets and food animals like chickens and pigs on deck, cultivating small gardens in pots and boxes, is not even conceivable to most Americans. When all the temples and pagodas and restaurants and street peddlers and hawkers and quaint little herb shops have been seen and enjoyed and exclaimed over, Aberdeen, for my money, is still the "don't-miss" attraction of Hong Kong. I was to see a good bit more of it than I'd planned on this trip, but I didn't know that as I hired a sampan to ferry me out to the huge floating restaurant known as the Sea Palace to meet Kate Longley for dinner.

I was early, so I had a drink at the bar and looked out at the boat traffic in the channel beside the window, fully as bustling and busy as a street in the business district of a large American city, except these were not Buicks and Plymouths and SUVs, but junks, sampans, rafts, and an occasional powerboat.

I suppose it was how different the Orient was that got to me. I've been to Rome and London, and if you ignored the landmarks like the Coliseum and closed your ears to the strange language, much of Europe resembles older sections of cities in the Midwestern part of America. But in Asia, where everyone looks different, the smell in the air is unique, and the customs and lifestyle and fashions are exotic and unfamiliar and quaint, you know you're not in Cleveland. Hong Kong is a vast and unending assault on the senses.

In the mirror I saw Katherine Longley come through the entryway. She looked around, then saw me and made her way to the bar, her height and carriage and honey-blond hair turning every head in her wake. I stood to greet her and she offered me her cheek. It was soft, and smelled good.

"Did you have a good day at the keyhole, dear?" she said after I'd secured a drink for her.

I laughed. "I learned a hell of a lot, although I'm not sure it has anything to do with Jake. Want to hear?"

She nodded eagerly, like a little girl.

"Averell Brown is running some sort of a con game with this so-called movie he's going to produce, and Jimmy Yee is his target. Duncan McLoughlin and Lloyd Sturdevant are bankrolling Yee, at least part of the way."

She sipped her Kir thoughtfully. "I can't say I'm surprised about Brown, but I am about Jimmy Yee. He's a smart man—that's how he got so rich. One wouldn't think he could be played for a fool."

"Everyone in the world is an expert on two subjects, Kate—their own business, and show business. For a man like Jimmy Yee, who revels in his wealth and power, the idea of being the boss of bosses on a movie must seem irresistible. I'm sure Brown tempted him with visions of willing starlets, and the whole idea of chumming around with Denzel Washington or Tom Cruise would have earned him lots of face. Anybody can make money, but how many can invite Tom Cruise to dinner?"

"Oh, my," she said.

"It's all right—that's the way a lot of films get financed. For the most part, though, vanity and ego are what makes movies happen, which is why there are so many lousy movies. It's unfortunate that some really unscrupulous operators like Brown don't even make the damn picture—they just take the front money and pocket it. And he must have figured that it's somehow easier to find a plump and yetunplucked pigeon outside the United States."

My name was called over the loudspeaker and we were ushered to our table. Kate had requested one by a window, and we ate oysters stir-fried with ginger and scallions, a delicious garlic crab I'd only recommend if one doesn't plan on being kissed for several days, and a dessert called almond jelly that was so sweet it made my teeth ache.

After dinner we repaired back to the bar for cognacs to get rid of the sugary taste.

"Where do you go from here?" Kate asked. "You don't seem to have anything concrete."

"Nothing I could take to court, no. But there's financial hanky-panky, I'm sure of that, and big money turns lots of us into creatures of nightmare. I still have a few people I want to talk to."

She raised her eyebrows, waiting to hear who they were.

"Police Superintendent Eckhard, for one."

"Cock Robin?" she said, and I had to laugh. Robin Eckhard, who was also a drinking chum of Jake's, was Hong Kong's most dedicated womanizer. He revels in the nickname.

"I'll drop by headquarters and see him tomorrow. But tonight, if you wouldn't mind, I'd like to have a nightcap at the Godown."

It's remarkable the way that the very structure of a human face seems to change when someone hits a sensitive spot in the psyche. The transformation of Kate Longley's lovely features at that moment was indeed remarkable. I have been known to push people's buttons deliberately—sometimes because of my job and sometimes because I can be pretty malicious—but this had been inadvertent, and I wondered what the secret word had been that caused the duck to drop.

"I'll pass, thank you. Just drop me off home and you're welcome to the car." The ice in her voice could have serviced an entire pitcher of margaritas.

I was tired of floundering around blindly and occasionally stepping on a land mine, so I decided to press it. "I hate wandering around alone," I said. "Besides, there will be people there you know, I'm sure. You can introduce me. It'll save a lot of time." And then, to soften it, "And I don't particularly want to let you go just yet."

"I'm afraid you'll have to if you're heading for the Godown. I don't go in there."

"Why not?"

The fire and anger from deep within flared to the surface. "I just don't, that's all!" Then, more quietly, "Don't push me." It was more entreaty than threat.

I took a shot in the dark. "Stanley Nivens?"

Tears welled up in her eyes suddenly, and I could see her struggle for control. "How did you know?"

"Last night you clammed up when his name was mentioned. Today you told me you'd been involved with someone and it ended badly. I just fit the pieces together and took a guess."

The sound she made was perilously close to a whimper. "It was a good one. Stanley and I were together for a long time. He's the most charming man in the world if he hasn't had too much to drink, and I loved him dearly. He hurt me very badly, and the wounds haven't had time to form protective scabs yet, that's all." She shook her head as if to clear it. "I'm sorry. I didn't mean to dump all my woes on you."

I reached over and touched her face with the back of my hand; it felt warm and flushed. "If it helps at all, I think Stanley is a stupid asshole to let you go."

"That is the nicest thing I can think of to say about Stanley Nivens at the moment."

After we finished our drinks I drove her back to the flat. I had grave misgivings about letting her go this evening, but fighting down my attraction to her in favor of helping to find out what happened to Jake McKay was something I was becoming accustomed to.

I held onto her hand a few seconds longer than was absolutely necessary before she got out of the car. "I may punch Stanley right in the nose when I meet him."

"Please don't do that," she said. "Every relationship inevitably ends in one of three ways—you get married, someone ends it, or one person dies. There are no other alternatives. Things being how they are these days, most people break up."

"Look," I said, feeling guilty about the whole business, "I shouldn't be too long. I just want to ask some questions around people who know Jake well. Wait up for me and we'll have a brandy when I get home. Please?"

"On one condition."

"Anything."

"Don't even mention Stanley's name to me."

"Stanley who?" I said.

Driving her Nissan back over the Peak was no mean feat for me. For years I had driven an Alfa Romeo convertible, so I was at ease with sports cars, but I was not accustomed to driving on the left side of the road. I was relieved there was no one in the car with me and that there was little Sunday evening traffic, because my wild gyrations in getting used to the English way of driving made me a prime candidate for poster boy of the uncoordinated. It took a lot of concentration, and I was damp at the armpits by the time I got back to the Central District.

The Godown was in a little alleyway, marked by a bright white overhead light bulb and the presence of a large, bearded and be-turbanned Pakistani doorman, who made no effort to open the door for me but stared glumly at me as I walked in. Hong Kong was one of those places where everyone fit into neat pigeonholes. The Aberdeen boat people were Hokla Chinese, the restaurants were mostly owned and staffed by émigrés from the province of Canton, wealthy manufacturers like Jimmy Yee were mostly from Taiwan, import and export mavens were Australian or New Zealanders—'En-Zeds' as the British called them—and the doormen were all Pakistani or 'Paks' for short. The tourist trade was partly American and partly Japanese, to whom the Yanks had surrendered their image of jingoistic and omnipresent camera-clickers who loudly demanded the kind of service they never got back home.

I settled down in a booth against the wall and looked around for a friendly face, but no one seemed to pay much attention to me, figuring I was a tourist who was slumming. It was a lonely feeling when I noticed the conviviality of the large group of men and women sitting on either side of a long refectory table in the middle of the room. When the rather spiky Australian waitress, who was wearing a gilded razor blade around her neck on a chain, brought my Courvoisier, I asked her if Stanley Nivens was among the group. She pointed him out and I took my drink over to where he sat.

He looked up. "Cheerio," he said brightly, and it was the vacancy of his grin that told me he was completely ripped. When I identified myself as a friend of Jake McKay's, he pumped my hand heartily and offered to introduce me to the rest of his group.

"Thanks," I said, "but maybe later. Right now I wonder if we might talk alone."

He looked a bit puzzled, but agreed and got unsteadily to his feet. I had to help him back to my booth.

Stanley Nivens was a very tall man, perhaps six foot three, and from the look of him somewhere around sixty. A lifetime of hard drinking had sketched a red network of ruptured blood vessels on his nose, and there was a hangdog slack to his jowls and the corners of his full mouth. In contrast was a boyish, innocent look in his eyes denoting the total acceptance, indeed the celebration, of his alcohol habit. He wore a dashing mustache that went well with the wrinkled khaki field jacket and the badly tied ascot around his neck, and his hair was a glossy black, setting off his green eyes and giving him the rakehell foreign-correspondent look I'm sure he was striving for.

When he spoke he displayed a stuffy, upper class Colonel Blimp British accent that was almost impossible to understand, and I wasn't convinced it was only his advanced state of inebriation that caused me to catch only key phrases. For all his booziness, Stanley had a certain boyish charm, and his man-of-the-world aura must have seemed very glamorous to a woman like Kate.

I explained to him that I had come to Hong Kong to help find Jake McKay.

"Yes, Jake," he mumbled. "Missing, eh? Unlikely, what? What? Yes, Jake's aces, absolutely topper. Best friend I've got in the ruddy world, you s'm." That seemed to trouble him, as if he had suddenly realized he didn't have that many friends. "Well, how do you come to me, then? Kate, I'll wager. Hmm, good old gel, Kate. She must be a bit ragged about me still, eh? Can't really blame her much." He called for another neat whiskey, and the waitress brought it right over. "Suppose I used Kate rather shabbily, didn't I? Sorry, hmm."

"Stanley, can you remember the last time you saw Jake?"

He frowned, trying to remember, and the tug he took on his whiskey wasn't going to aid his memory. I could almost hear the wheels turning and grinding in his head as he fought his way through the fog of alcohol fumes that must have been enveloping his brain. "Don't know for certain," he said with a kind of awe at the realization of his own mental deterioration. "Monday? Tuesday? The days all run together, you s'm." By now I had figured out that "you s'm" was his own, quaint, playing-field-of-Eton way of articulating "you see," but the rest of his speech was still a bitch for me to decipher.

"Do you remember where it was you saw him?"

"Right here," he said. "We were getting pissed together, is all. As usual."

I spoke slowly, as though to a child who wasn't paying attention. "Now Stanley, think very hard. When you were drinking together, did Jake say anything about his boat? About taking a trip?"

"His boat. Damn shame, what? Someone copping his boat like that. He loved it. *The Hong Kong Lady.* Treated it like his child. No, he wasn't going anywhere in particular on her. Too drunk to drive, much less go sailing around in the South China Sea. Like me. Too drunk to drive. Too drunk to do much of anything." He looked right at me and his bloodshot eyes focused for a moment. "I drink all the time, you s'm. Drink and fuck and file dispatches to the paper back home. Rather an interesting life, what? What? And nobody gives a shit for any of it. 'Cept Jake. Good old boy, Jake, what? Bloody hell!"

Another sip of his drink and his eyes dimmed again and

got a little more red. Talking to him was a waste of time at this stage of his binge. I helped him out of the booth and piloted him toward the men's room like a tug guiding a large freighter into harbor. Then I left.

As things turned out, I probably should have stayed longer.

I had parked at the garage in the Conrad International, so decided to take a shortcut back from the Godown across Chater Garden. It was a cool night, and I buttoned my jacket against the chill as I saw a diminutive Chinese man approaching. I thought nothing of the fact that he was heading right for me. I assumed he was a street beggar, or that he wanted to sell me something.

"Good evening, sir," he said. "You rike the company of young rady?"

Most of the pimps I had seen in Los Angeles were young, mostly black, and generally well over six feet tall, dressed in velveteen jump suits and beaver hats and four inch high boots, dripping with gold jewelry. This man was in his late fifties, wearing a cheap sports jacket and wrinkled plaid pants, and couldn't have stood over four feet ten. A mini-pimp.

I looked down almost paternally at him and shook my head no.

Now, I'm not one of those raving paranoiacs who think everyone who's out on the street after sunset is a mugger or a sex maniac or has some other evil purpose in mind. I don't walk the nighttime streets with a hatpin in my fist or a handful of pepper in my pocket, and I always figure those people who carry a vial of mace spray are just asking to have it taken away from them by an assailant and used against them. I've wandered the darks of many places with little thought for my own safety, too busy drinking in the sights and sounds of the city that stimulate and excite me. But some inner sense—call it radar or clairvoyance or whatever instinct it is that has kept me alive and intact for almost fifty years—made me turn around just in time to see a Chinese youth wearing a satiny gang-type jacket with a snarling tiger appliquéd on the back, aim a prodigious karate chop at my head.

The turn caused the blow to miss its original mark, but it did glance off my shoulder rather painfully. I gathered my feet under my weight quickly. The kid was still off-balance from throwing the chop and missing, and I put a lot of steam into the short uppercut I aimed at his nose. I scored a bull's-eye, feeling bone and cartilage crunch against my knuckles. His head snapped back as the blood spurted from his nostrils and I saw his eyes go silly. He jerked backwards onto the grass, knocking all the wind out of his lungs when he landed, and then he scrambled unsteadily to his feet and took off, running like hell in the general direction of the wa-terfront with only one frightened and disoriented glance at me over his shoulder. I whirled around to face the little man, who was now holding a not-so-little knife, but when he took one look at me, ready for him and obviously willing to do him damage, he had second thoughts. He turned and scurried away in the opposite direction, toward Queen's Road.

I stood there in the middle of the pocket park feeling ex-posed and violated and I suppose a little stupid. I wouldn't have risked walking through a park at night in an American city, for all my lack of concern with night people and their rapacious ways, but I had traveled halfway around the world to become the near-victim of an old-fashioned Eighth Avenue mugging.

Now belatedly cautious, I looked around, checking out

the terrain in all directions, before continuing on to the Conrad International. My stride had changed, my whole attitude was guarded and fearful, and then I remembered that a professional mugger could read the body language of an intended mark to ascertain whether or not it would be a good idea to pull any rough stuff, and I stood up a bit straighter and began walking with confidence and a hint of aggression.

I wiped the young kid's nose blood from my hand with a handkerchief and threw it into a trash basket before crossing the streetcar tracks on Queen's Road, and it didn't register with me until I'd rescued Kate's car and was driving back to her place in Repulse Bay that, with so many small and elderly Japanese tourists roaming the side streets of Hong Kong with their expensive cameras and bulging wallets, these particular muggers had chosen to attack a very tall, rather muscular American within three hundred yards of the Conrad International Hotel.

Chapter Five

I owe a couple of sticks of incense to whichever of the numerous Chinese gods it was whose purview included having Boomer Crane already asleep when I arrived back at the flat. Not only was I in no mood for a lot of jocular Southern-fried machismo, I was delighted at having Kate all to myself.

She was waiting for me in a long black and gold robe of fine Thai silk, wearing a subtle patchouli scent, her hair fastened away from her face with two barrettes, and looking dizzyingly sexy. The teapot whistled merrily with boiling water with which to steam the brandy glasses, and a very tasty recording by the late Cal Tjader was playing on the sound system. I don't believe she meant to create such a highly charged atmosphere; maybe it was just me.

It often is.

She was looking a bit tense nonetheless, but I surmised that was because she knew I'd been talking to Stanley Nivens, a subject we carefully avoided as per our pre-arrangement. I didn't tell her about my near-mugging—there was no point in upsetting her. She was, however, vastly amused by my tale of difficulty in driving her left-handed car.

"If we put you in the fast lane of the Santa Monica Freeway during rush hour, you'd be singing a different tune, my pretty," I told her. The brandy was mellowing me out and striking just the right balance.

"I'm sure that's meant to be extremely threatening, but since I haven't an inkling as to what the Santa—what?—Santa Monica Freeway is all about, I'm afraid it loses its bite."

"Never been to the U.S.?"

"Never. The exotic east fits in more with my girlhood fantasies, so when I decided to make the break with family and tradition, I headed this way."

She sipped her brandy thoughtfully. Kate had a way of lapping at a drink with the end of her tongue that made me want to bite it. "Did you have any luck today?"

"I don't know, Kate. I've only been here one day and already half of Hong Kong is mad at me. And that means that I'll probably turn Jake up pretty soon. Don't worry, I won't leave here until I do."

She smiled at me over the rim of her glass. "You care for him very much, don't you?"

I nodded. "He's an irresponsible bounder and a tosspot, and he likes hiding from the rest of the world he grew up in, but friends like Jake don't happen every day, and when they do you value and cherish them and come to their aid when the need arises."

"I don't imagine friends like you come along every day, either."

I shrugged. "There are at least fifty people who would tell you I'm a selfish, egotistical shit, and they'd probably be right. But Jake is special. There're only a few people like him."

"A fortunate few, I'd say, to have such a loyal friend."

I lowered my lashes to accept the compliment. Then I looked back up at her. I was seated on the low sofa, and she was opposite me in a high-backed wing chair. "What about you, Kate? What is a bright, beautiful woman like you doing ten thousand miles from hearth and home in what's now Communist China, playing den mother to an expatriate actor and a hired killer?"

She blinked. "Don't you think you're being a bit harsh on poor Boomer?"

"And poor Kate, too?"

She sighed. "Me? I don't know. My family is in Leeds—middle class, Anglican Church country gentry. It was all so—brown. I was bored. I wanted some excitement, I wanted to see the fleshpots of the world. I've worked my way all over the Pacific Rim—Jakarta, Manila, Singapore. Finally I thought I'd give Hong Kong a look before returning home to marry the vicar and become a house mouse. So I arrived here, and I became—involved. I've stayed too long at the fair, I suppose, and now it's become home, or what passes for it. I hate it here now, but I've come too far to go back." She forced a smile. "A bit of an impasse, wouldn't you say?"

"What about Europe?"

She laughed. "How very American of you, Anthony! I was born in Europe. To me, the rest of Europe is where one goes for the weekend. No thank you. I imagine I'll stay on here a bit until I can think of somewhere else to go."

"There's always Bangkok," I said.

This time she didn't look away until almost ten seconds had passed. Finally she said, "You must be exhausted. There's a telly in Jake's room, if you didn't notice it last night. He loves to watch American shows dubbed into Cantonese. It puts him to sleep."

I stood up and she did, too, and I put my hands on her arms just above the elbows. "I'm going to find him, Kate."

"I know you will. I have every confidence in you." The silk of her robe whispered as she moved to the hallway with me, and at the door to Jake's room she turned her cheek for me to kiss goodnight. I chose a different target, and while she didn't exactly pull away, her lips were unresponsive. I pulled back and she shook her head; whether she was telling me no or telling herself, I wasn't sure. She put her fingertips on my lips, and it took all my willpower to keep from licking them.

"Please don't confuse me," she said. "I'm still on the walking wounded list."

"All right, I won't. But it's getting to be about time you let go of the past. If not me, okay, but you're too good to spend the rest of your life in hiding."

"Are you sure?"

"Of what?"

"That I'm too good. You don't know. I might be a cold bitch, an emotional cripple, and a sexual washout."

"That's a bet I'd like to take," I said softly, and as she started to protest I overrode her. "Okay, then—not now. You have sweet dreams."

"My father used to say that."

"Great. The very image I was looking for."

"I didn't mean it like that. I just—look, I like you. You're a nice man, and you're very attractive. Your timing's rotten, that's all." She put a hand on my cheek. "Ciao," she said, and she was gone down the corridor with that suggestive whisk of silk, the aroma of patchouli and the feel of fingers on lips an enduring ghost where she'd stood.

I went into Jake's room, undressed, and got into bed, memorizing every imperfection in the ceiling, lost in longing like an unfulfilled adolescent coming home from his first date with a raging case of blue balls. My fantasy of her changing her mind and stealing into my room in the middle of the night with her silk robe singing was not realized, and I finally dropped off to sleep disappointed, my worry about Jake troubling my rest. It was the kind of sleep that doesn't do you much good; my REM must have been going a mile a minute.

Early the next morning I called police headquarters and

made an appointment for later that day with CID Superintendent Robin Eckhard, who seemed delighted to hear from me and invited me to lunch at the Mandarin Hotel. I was on my second cup of coffee, enjoying the view of Repulse Bay out the window, when Kate came out of her room, looking very efficient and professional in a dark blue suit and a white blouse. I offered to pour her some coffee, but she said she had to run. It was as though the previous night had never happened, and after she left I thought back over it and realized that not much had really transpired. I hadn't exactly made a pass; I'd only tried for one kiss, and she had gently said no. I tried not to think of why I was making so much of it in my mind.

About ten minutes after she left, I heard a key in the front door, and Boomer Crane came bouncing in. It had never occurred to me that he wasn't asleep in his room. He was wearing a sweatsuit and running shoes; he was an early-morning jogger, like one of those silly people one sees perspiring along the side of the highway, running in place at red lights and looking fashionable in their Adidas running suits and terrycloth headbands and Walkman headphones, wearing the smug expression of the self-righteous, exhibiting a certain scorn for those of us in our cars who perhaps didn't take such exquisite care of our own bodies and who polluted the air they felt entitled to by birthright with our noxious exhaust fumes. Boomer had the beach at Repulse Bay for his jogging track, so at least he couldn't be blamed for being a traffic hazard.

After I declined his invitation to join him in shin splints and stitches in the side the next morning, he informed me that he'd be heading into Central after his shower and that he'd give me a lift. I thought for a while about declining, wondering whether I wouldn't prefer the company of a silent Chinese taxi driver, but I finally said yes, and washed up the coffee cups while he showered and dressed.

"I hear you had a run-in with Fat-Ass Brown at the Pen yesterday morning," he said when we were finally under way in his black Hyundai. "You better watch yourself with him. That's a bad nigger."

"I know," I said. "All the good ones are field hands and shoe shine boys."

He gave me a disdainful look. "A limousine liberal, huh? Knock it off, will you? It's just an expression."

"So are redneck and shit-kicker."

He remained unoffended. "Okay, fine. That's what I am. I'm not ashamed of it. I played ball with a lot of colored boys, I'm no bigot. But we are what we are, though, and there's no point in calling it something else."

"I just don't happen to like that word, that's all."

"Well, what would *you* call Averell Brown?"

"I don't want to argue either race or semantics with you, Boomer. It's too nice a morning."

"Glad to hear it. Any leads on Jake yet?"

"Nothing concrete. But there's lots of strange stuff going on in this town and it all seems to point back to Averell Brown. Whether or not Jake is involved in it is something I haven't figured out yet."

"Everybody's got a story here, Holton. This is the Far East. You can theorize all you want, but the fact is that old Jake was a nosy fucker. Always poking around in other people's business just for the hell of it."

"I don't like the past tense, Boomer."

"Neither do I, but I don't like sticking my head in the sand, either. Because when you do that, it means your ass is sticking up in the air."

"Did Jake ever stick his nose into your business?"

He nodded. "Mine, Kate's, everybody's. It's probably what made him such a good actor—intellectual curiosity. The way I figure it, he found out something he shouldn't have and somebody took him out."

"That's pretty cold."

"I don't like the idea any more than you, but you gotta be realistic. Brown may seem like a fat clown to you, just like I might seem like an overgrown Bubba. I think you like to pigeonhole people that way. I frankly don't give owl shit whether you like me or not, but Brown isn't just comic relief around here. I heard of him in Johannesburg a few years back. He was pretty heavy into smuggling."

"Guns?"

"Diamonds. I hear he used to sneak them out of the country by putting them up his ass. The word is, if he ever sets foot on the African continent again he won't live two hours. He was a pretty heavy dude, and I don't mean his weight."

"You think this movie deal of his is a cover-up?"

"Hell, I don't know anything. I'm just an old country boy." His exaggerated drawl affected me like fingernails on a blackboard. "I'm just telling you that you haven't even started digging yet, and when you do, there's no telling what you're gonna dig up."

We were approaching the Mandarin Hotel, and he slowed the car. "You've got one thing wrong, Boomer. I don't think you're a dumb shit-kicker. Or a dumb anything. That would be a bad miscalculation."

"It would at that. But you don't like me much," he said pleasantly.

"I don't like your type, and you play that to the hilt. Also, I'm not sure I trust you."

"That makes us even all around, because I don't like

your type either. But if you ever decide that you need me for anything—*anything*—I'm here to help. I mean that."

He held out his meaty paw for me to shake before I got out of the car, and this time, although his grip was still strong and firm, he didn't try to pulverize my fingers. I suppose that was his way of declaring a truce. I couldn't decide whether the animosity we obviously felt for one another was only that of two Alpha males or whether it was something else a lot more dangerous.

Chapter Six

Robin Eckhard was waiting for me at the bar of the restaurant on the top floor of the hotel, passing the time with an attractive, dark-haired Englishwoman who, he told me later, had come to Asia with her husband on a business trip and was bored silly. Before leaving with me for our table, he gave her his business card and promised to show her the sights and wonders of Hong Kong. Handsome, blond, with a little wispy mustache and suiting by Saville Row, he lived up to his nickname of Cock Robin.

The management had been holding a table by the window for us. As Deputy Superintendent of the CID, he was well known and probably a little feared by everyone on the Hong Kong side. As soon as we sat down I took advantage of the view as Victoria Harbour spread out before us. Dominating the panorama was a curious-looking building, a tall white monolith with round porthole-like windows.

Eckhard saw me looking. "That's the Connaught Centre," he said. "You know what the Chinese call it? The House of a Thousand Assholes."

I laughed. "Because of the round windows."

"Only partly. It's supposedly jinxed. Did you notice the steel awning all around the building just above street level? Pieces of the building fall off from time to time, and for a while it got so bad that they put up the awning to keep pedestrians from getting killed."

"Bad construction?"

"Bad *feng shui*."

"Help me out, Robin, my Chinese is only good enough to ask for the men's room."

"*Feng shui*," he said. "A noble and ancient science. The

80

Chinese believe that there is a dragon that lives under the earth. Well, I'm not sure if they really believe it, but this is the story. When you build a house or a building, you have to make sure it isn't resting on the dragon's eye or his spine or his balls or anyplace else that will make him uncomfortable, because you don't want to cheese off a dragon. So they hire *feng shui* men, men who supposedly know about these things, and they'll do their nonsense and then tell you that you must build the structure eight feet or four feet or whatever north of where you originally planned or the dragon's going to get you."

"You're joking."

"The powers-that-were who put up that building aren't laughing. They felt a *feng shui* man was an unnecessary expense, so they went ahead without one and built the Connaught the way they wanted to. I guess the dragon didn't like it, because first the windows would blow out in a strong wind—and we have a lot of those during *taifun* season. Then after a while, great hunks of the building's facade started dropping off and beaning passersby. They tried re-facing the entire building and that didn't work, so eventually they gave up and put up the steel awning.

"You're not telling me you believe that crap?"

He shrugged. "The official verdict is that the Connaught has bad *feng shui*. Who am I to argue with a dragon?"

He signaled the waiter and we ordered lunch. Then he turned serious. "I suppose you've come here to find Jake?"

"You know about it?"

"There are no secrets on this island, old sock, especially from the CID. Jake came to me about his boat when she first went missing, but there wasn't much I could do about it."

"Why not?"

"Well, she's not on the island, that's for sure. And if she's not, she's out of my jurisdiction."

"You know that no one's seen Jake for several days?"

He nodded. "I did some checking on Saturday. He didn't fly out of here, and he didn't take the train from Kowloon into the New Territories or the PRC. So he's either still on the island or he's left by sea. If he's still alive, that is."

I suppressed a shudder. "You have a theory."

"Don't laugh."

"I won't."

"Pirates," he said. "Not your Captain Kidd types with peg legs and parrots and eye patches. But piracy in Asia is as common as marijuana in Los Angeles. I imagine that's what happened to *The Hong Kong Lady*."

"And what happened to Jake?"

"That might be a bit more dicey."

"I've done some asking around," I said.

He held up an interrupting hand. "I know that, too. I'm way ahead of you. I heard about your little tête-à-tête with Averell Brown minutes after it happened."

"So tell me."

"What?"

"Start with Brown."

"He's a twit," Eckhard said scornfully. He took out a notebook and flipped some pages. "Averell Brown, born New York City forty-four years ago. Did some time in juvenile hall for running policy slips and beating up slow-pay debtors in Harlem. He grew up on the streets, and went to Africa and fell in with the Nelson Mandela crowd for a time until they got wise to him and kicked his arse out. He found his way to Capetown and went into diamond smuggling rather substantially, first as muscle and later as a courier.

They say he got millions in uncut stones out of the country and dumped them all on the London and Amsterdam markets. The thought of flying from Johannesburg to London with an uncut diamond up my bum isn't pleasant, but for Brown I suppose the rewards justified it."

"Did he eventually get caught?"

"Not by the authorities, no. But he supposedly double-crossed those he was working for—nicked them for about a million pounds, they say. He's out of the diamond business now, or anything else in Africa. The South African authorities want him, his former associates want him even more."

"So he came here?"

"Not directly. He went to Los Angeles first and got in with the movie folk in some way. I guess that's how he knew Jake McKay. But they probably caught on to his bullshit early on. The next thing anyone knew, he was here in Hong Kong, living in a rented mansion up on the mid-levels and making noises about producing a big expensive film. It's a scam, we think, but so far he's done nothing we can arrest him for. So we're watching him closely and hoping we can keep him alive when the Chinese finally figure he's having the rise on them."

"You think Jake was threatening to queer his action and he took him out?"

He looked at me levelly. "No. Jake is your friend, but you don't know him on a day-to-day basis like I do. Jake's is a policy of *laissez-faire,* which by the way is the only possible method of existence in this city. As long as you're square with Jake, he wouldn't care if you were into opium trading or white slavery or buggering sheep. Besides, he has that actor's mentality—and there was a possibility, however slim, of a good role in a big film and lots of money for him. And for that he'd probably play ball with the devil himself.

Moreover, Brown needed Jake as well, for credibility, for proof to the Chinese that he was okay with the Hollywood crowd. Brown is a wanker, and I've no doubt he's been responsible for a certain amount of population-reduction in his African days, but I don't think he'd want to hurt Jake McKay."

"Fair enough. What about Jimmy Yee?"

"Jimmy's a shark. Tycoon. Financial wizard. Entrepreneur. And he keeps several little whores stashed in flats that he owns, mostly on the Kowloon side. Around here, married men seem to think that if they live on the Hong Kong side, all they have to do is cross the harbor to play and their wives won't know. The wives do, of course, but they don't let on. It's a matter of face."

"Do you know how heartily sick I am of face?"

"Hard cheese, old man, because you happen to be sitting in the bloody face capital of the world."

"Would Jimmy Yee have any reason to want Jake out of the way?"

"I don't know. He certainly has the wherewithal. Anyone that rich and powerful has only to pick up the telephone and you'd be feeding the fishes off Shek-O. But Jimmy prefers squeezing your balls financially. I'd say murder is way out of character for him."

"What about Lloyd Sturdevant and Duncan McLoughlin?"

Eckhard made a face. "Are you going to vet the bona fides of everyone in bloody Hong Kong? That's a lifetime job. Remember, ninety percent of the Caucasians in Asia are ex-pats. Expatriates. Some of your Yanks stayed over here after Vietnam. They were fellows who were in dead-end marriages and dead-end jobs at home, they took to the mysterious East, and decided to stay. And it was easier to let people think they were MIAs. They assumed new identities, most of them. In Asia it's quite a simple matter to pick up a new passport, especially an Australian one. So they open up a store or a bar or they run guns to the rebels—doesn't matter which rebels, there are always plenty to go round—and they set up housekeeping with some little slant-eyed doll who waits on them hand and foot and puts up with their possibly weird sexual fetishes that would send an American princess screaming home to her mum. And they rake in the coin a lot faster and easier than if they'd gone back home to pump petrol in Alabama."

"And pretty soon," I said, "even they forget who they used to be."

"Exactly. Asia is a superb place in which to hide for the rest of your life, and there are some things even we all-knowing and all-seeing coppers can't get a handle on."

"Sturdevant and McLoughlin," I said doggedly.

"Ah, the Gold Dust Twins." He turned to another page in his notebook. "This is what we have, but I don't guarantee its veracity, especially on Sturdevant. As far as we know, he was a fancy sleight-of-hand artist in the U.S. securities market during the late eighties and early nineties, and he was a half step away from taking up residence in one of those country club prisons your government reserves for very rich people who have been naughty. So he decided to move his base of operations over here. There's a good reason for that. The financial and banking structure over here has always been rather loose. We're the last bastion of *laissez-faire* capitalism left in the world, Communist Chinese notwithstanding. The laws here allow a good deal that wouldn't be tolerated in the U.S. or Europe. A fellow like Sturdevant can do his dog-and-pony act perfectly legally here and still be a respected member of the community.

85

Which he is, by the way. He belongs to all the right clubs, he's on several boards, including that of the Canton Bank. Again, we're keeping a sharp eye on him, but at the moment he's just a slick but legitimate operator who's brought a lot of capital onto the island. Personally I think he's a wanker, but we can't arrest a chap because we don't like the cut of his jib, even here in primitive and uncivilized Asia. He's quite a sailor, too—and he works hard at it."

"McLoughlin a big money type, too?"

Eckhard took a long French cigarette from a gold case and lit it with a gold lighter I don't think he bought on a policeman's pay. "Duncan McLoughlin is another story. He seems to be an organized crime guy, a London bully-boy."

"What's he doing here, then?"

"Riding Sturdevant's coattails, from what we can gather. He brought a good bit of the coin of the realm over here with him, but he doesn't say much. He rather hovers about in Sturdevant's shadow. He's at the race track a lot."

"I've been told that they wanted *The Hong Kong Lady* rather desperately. Do you know why?"

"Probably because it's a damn fine boat. They seem to be very competitive men, especially Sturdevant. He's quite vain about his sailing, and I suppose it burned them that a mere film actor had a boat that could leave their own floundering in its wake. But they don't have to steal. They're too rich."

"Let's say they don't have to steal, but they chose to. Do you suppose that somehow Jake caught them with their pants down and that they wanted him out of the way?"

"Anything is possible. But you must remember that this is a city built on corruption and greed and double-shuffles, and those that aren't con men or manipulators or thieves or pirates are usually Yank spies or Russian spies or spies for Christ Almighty knows who else. Everyone else is a coolie."

"Diogenes would have run out of lamp oil in Hong Kong," I said.

"Come off it. You know damn well that everyone who's successful and powerful has his own particular vices, and some of them can be downright disgusting. We're just more open about it here, that's all."

A uniformed page boy came walking through the restaurant, wearing a short brass-buttoned coat and little pillbox hat like the dwarf who used to "call for Philip Morris" cigarettes back in the forties. He held an old-fashioned slate on the end of a long stick, atop which was a little tinkling bell, and written across the slate was my name. It was a good thing, too, because I never would have made "Holton" out of whatever it was the boy was saying.

"You're being paged, I believe," Eckhard said. "The phones are in the foyer."

I tipped the boy with a ten-dollar Hong Kong note and threaded my way through the tables to the bank of telephones near the elevator.

It was Kate.

"I knew you were seeing Robin, so I phoned police headquarters and they told me where you were."

"Is something wrong, Kate?"

"I don't know. Johnson Lau called me here at the office wanting very much to contact you. He said you should call him at the Yacht Club." She gave me the number.

"Dinner tonight?"

"I thought I'd cook in. I have some excellent steaks from Japan."

"I didn't travel all this way to eat steak. Let me take you out for an elegant Chinese dinner somewhere."

"I'd really rather eat in. Boomer won't be here. He's flying to Manila tonight."

"Steak it is," I said quickly.

I hung up and dialed the Yacht Club, and after a few moments Johnson Lau came to the phone.

"I thought you might like to take a little boat ride," he said, coming to the point quickly in a most un-Chinese fashion.

"Oh?"

"I'll show you our sights, including some that most tourists don't get to see." The urgency in his voice told me he didn't want to get any more specific over the phone.

"All right, when?" I said.

"Miss Longley said you were having lunch with Superintendent Eckhard."

"Yes, I'm with him now."

"How long will you be?"

"Give me two hours."

"Excellent. Meet me here at the club then. And Mr. Holton—just between the two of us, heya?"

"Of course. Thank you, Johnson. I'll be there."

I went back to the table, but Robin was three tables away, talking to two attractive European women. He laid business cards on both of them and came back to his seat.

"Trouble?" he asked.

"Not at all. You?"

"Hardly." He smiled over at the two women, and they smiled back. "Where were we?"

"Having a meaningless discussion on geographical morality. Can we get back to the problem of Jake McKay?"

"Your single-mindedness can be tiresome."

"Missing friends do that to me. What about Jake's flat-mate?"

"Which one?"

I hesitated. "Both of them. Let's start with Boomer Crane."

"Obnoxious nickname, don't you think? In his own mind he was one of your football greats, but the reality of it was a bit different. He played at university, I gather, and that's about all. He's become a mercenary since then, although he dabbles in import-export, and he's been involved in all sorts of seamy little revolutions all over the globe. His moral convictions begin and end at his checkbook."

"I know all that. Anything else?"

"That's quite enough, don't you think?"

"Would he have any reason to steal the boat?"

"Hardly, he sails it as much as Jake. Besides, he's frankly not sharp enough to have pulled it off."

"Anything else? Any motive for wanting Jake dead?"

"Jake has the bigger bedroom, but that's hardly grounds for murder. They sailed together because Boomer is damned good at it, and I suppose they got along all right, but they aren't really close friends. They have a good working relationship."

"Was Boomer into anything that he shouldn't have been? He said something about Jake sticking his nose where it didn't belong."

"Boomer Crane's activities are such an open book that he advertises his services in several publications, including the *South China Morning Post*. He makes no bones about what he is or what he does. As for the rest of it, he probably meant that he and Jake were at loggerheads over some woman."

"Wouldn't that make Boomer angry?"

"Angry enough to punch Jake in the nose, which he did on one occasion. They had quite a dust-up outside the Godown about eight months ago over a travel agent from San Francisco. That's long been forgotten, though."

"Are you sure?"

Eckhard shrugged. "If casual boffing was a reason for murder, you and I both should be quite dead by now. As for Kate, there's nothing between her and Jake, or her and Boomer for that matter, except friendship. They're both rather protective of her, as a matter of fact. She was involved for a long time with a chap named Stanley Nivens, but that went to bits some months ago. You've spoken to him already." It wasn't a question.

"You do know everything that goes on here, don't you?"

"It's my job. Stanley is a classic case—what Graham Greene and Somerset Maugham used to call a remittance man—a fellow from a wealthy UK family who's a bit of a problem child. The paterfamilias sends him off to the Far East somewhere—Singapore, Malaysia, Hong Kong, India—and remits him a tidy sum each month to keep him the hell away from the old home grounds. An embarrassment to the family, don't you know?"

The waiter finally arrived with lunch, and Robin Eckhard dug in with flying chopsticks. I was pretty good with them, but he put me to shame. The lunch was superb, too—oyster beef with broccoli, and pungent noodles in a brown sauce with a fiery touch of Szechuan pepper oil.

"There are lots of remittance men in HK," he said through mouthfuls. "Embezzlers, weeny-waggers, poofs, whoremongers, or just plain drunks. Stanley fits into the last category. He holds a nominal job as a journalist, and he's actually done excellent work sometimes. He's covered a foreign war or two, and when he's called on, he dries out just enough to do his job well. He's in Burke's Peerage, or at least his family is. He's an earl or baron or such. The title goes back to the Norman Conquest."

He took a sip of Lapsang Souchong tea. "In any event, Kate and Stanley were together for a long time, but they broke up and there was a scandal."

"Tell me about that."

"Why?" he asked, eyes twinkling. "Are you investigating Kate?"

"Sometimes you're too damned smart, Robin."

"That's how I stay alive. All right, no extra charge. Stanley took up with a Chinese woman, which is considered bad form by both races here. Not only that, she was married, and when it happened her husband took their child and went off somewhere. I think you know the lady. Jackie Ho, the P.R. gal over at the Conrad International."

I sat there quietly, my chopsticks poised in mid-flight while my oyster beef got cold on the plate.

"I envy the son of a bitch, frankly. He has fabulous taste in women, I'm sure you'll agree. But it was a bad show all around. Stanley has become even more of an outcast than before, Jackie is a fallen woman in polite Chinese society, and poor Kate went into a blue funk she's not out of yet." He pointed a chopstick at my left eye. "If you have any plans in that area, for God's sake be gentle. Kate is a nice woman and she doesn't need another sodding buggy ride."

"I will admit the thought crossed my mind," I said.

"As well it should. She's stunning."

"But I'm still more interested in finding Jake. You know his boat boy?"

"Johnson? Indeed I do. He's going to be a very big man here when he grows up. He's got the Asian cunning with

91

the American know-how, and he's as well-connected as any Chinese on the island."

"Connected how?"

"His family. They're super-rich. And they're triads. Powerful criminal elements here in China, and Johnson Lau's people are among the biggest. Dope, gold, arms, whatever, they're into it. They sent Johnson off to the U.S. for an education and then brought him back here. I suppose they felt that times were changing and the old ways needed a bit of sprucing up. Johnson is a step toward legitimacy."

"Then why is he working as a boat boy?" I said. "Why isn't he in one of the big banks or trading houses?"

"The yachting crowd is one of the only cliques in Hong Kong society where a young Chinese is judged on his ability and not his slant eyes. Johnson's gotten to know most of the important British traders on a social basis, which will stand him in good stead when he finally decides where he wants to go. He crews for Jake because he's a Yank and not involved in the day-to-day games and fancy doings of the money markets. He stays more or less neutral and better able to pick his spot."

"I met him yesterday," I said, avoiding any mention of my upcoming boat trip. "He seems very loyal to Jake."

"He is, I'm sure. Jake treated him as an equal from the very start. They even go out pulling birds together every so often. Among the young swinging crowd the racism isn't nearly as pronounced as it is in more establishment circles."

"You don't think Johnson stole Jake's boat, then?"

"What in bloody hell would he do with it? A twenty-three year old Chinese running around in a luxury yacht anyone in the Pacific could recognize at twenty paces? He'd stand out like a Hassidic rabbi on the streets of Amman. No, old fellow, I fear you are flogging a *cheval morte*."

The busboy came and cleared away the remains of our meal and I declined Robin's offer of an after-lunch brandy. I had the feeling I would need to be clear-headed.

"Let me offer some advice," he said as we were preparing to leave, his expression and voice turning official and serious. "You're close to being in over your head here. We're on top of the McKay business, and we don't want you standing around wanking your winkle, getting in our way. You could get hurt, and you could get other people hurt as well!."

"I'm just asking questions so far."

"So far, yes."

"I can play hardball with the best, Robin."

"Is that one of your Yank colloquialisms? Fine. I don't know it. But I'll tell you this: wrapping yourself in the Stars and Stripes doesn't make you invulnerable to an ice pick at the base of your skull or a dollop of strychnine in your afternoon tea. Nor does it protect you from arrest and prosecution. I tell you this as a friend. People have been known to disappear without a trace in Hong Kong."

"I know," I said. "Jake McKay is one of them."

Robin Eckhard and I said our good-byes after lunch, and he went off to police headquarters while I hailed a taxi to take me to Aberdeen. My head was swimming with too much information and I couldn't seem to make anything fit together.

I was also thinking about the policeman's warning. I knew I might be playing with rough kids, and I knew Eckhard wanted me out of it so he could do his own snooping. The police had paid informants here as they do everywhere else in the world, and I was content to let Eckhard have any glory that might accrue with finding Jake. What I was not content to do was sit idly by while my friend was missing and in danger.

As I walked, a white Mercedes sedan driven by a young Chinese pulled up beside me at the curb. The windows were darkened, but the rear one zapped down electrically and Averell Brown's huge head emerged. "Hey, mother-fucker!" he called.

I strolled over to the car, thinking how easy it would be to hurt him with his head sticking out that way, how I could just push down on the back of his neck so the partially lowered window would catch him right across the throat. I didn't do it, however, more out of curiosity than anything else. I wanted to find out what was on his mind.

"Good day, Mr. Brown," I said.

"Don't you good day me. You got a big fucking mouth, Holton."

"The better to eat you with, my dear."

He didn't laugh; I hadn't expected him to. "Why you wanna go telling Jimmy Yee and the guys all those lies about me?"

"I didn't tell any lies."

"Damn! Why you tryin' to queer my action here? I never done nothing to you." A newfound thought narrowed his eyes. "It's because I'm black, isn't it?"

"Oh, come off the Booker T. Washington shit," I said, leaning down so I was more on a level with him. "I don't give a damn what color you are, you're still an asshole. And you can run any kind of con you want, I couldn't care less. I just want to find Jake."

"So do I," he bleated. "He's the only credibility I got left around here, thanks to you flappin' your gums."

I had the feeling I was talking to a whiny child. "You really want to help, Brown?"

He nodded.

"Then move over."

He heaved his bulk over in the seat and I opened the door and climbed into the back of the Mercedes. "Tell your driver to go around the block a few times while we talk," I said.

The Chinese chauffeur turned and looked over his shoulder. "I speak English, sir," he said rather frostily.

The car began moving slowly in traffic. I looked at Brown and made my voice hard and tough. "Now you level with me," I said. His eyes shifted in the manner of a man in a jam. "Do you know who Robin Eckhard is? He's Deputy Superintendent of the CID and I just had lunch with him. Now, I'm asking you or he can ask you."

Brown looked down at his ham-like thighs. His whole demeanor had changed from yesterday, probably because he knew Jimmy Yee was just a step from cutting off his balls and he was running scared. "I'm trying to get this movie funded," he began, but I cut him off with a karate chop in the air.

"Without the bullshit. You never produced a movie in your life."

"How many guys you know never produced a movie in their life and then they do?" he whined. "I needed to get with the big-money guys in this town, the big-money Chinese. They're not too hip to the Hollywood scene."

"So it is a scam?"

He looked away. "Not exactly."

"Okay, so you're a beautiful human being. Where does Jake McKay fit in?"

"I needed Jake to introduce me to these money people. He runs in their circles."

"Jimmy Yee?"

"That's who it turned out to be, yeah. Jake McKay is the reason I came here."

"I don't follow."

"How many world-class Hollywood actors like Jake are living off in some third world country running around with the yachting crowd? I needed Jake for respectability."

"How did you know Jake?"

"I didn't. I knew Boomer Crane."

The backs of my wrists prickled and I clenched my fists. Brown noticed and scooted farther away from me against his side of the car. He thought I was going to hit him. The thought had crossed my mind. "How did you and Boomer know each other?"

"Africa," he said. "We knew each other in Africa."

"Boomer doesn't much like black people."

"I don't much like redneck crackers, but business is business."

"You mean Boomer is in for some money?"

"Five percent right across the top, as finder's fee. A pretty good day's pay just for setting up a lunch. And even if the movie don't get made, he's still in for five percent of whatever I get out of it. He's already made five large."

"Are you trying to tell me Boomer set Jake up as your beard?"

The whites of his eyes glowed bright against the dark brown of his face in the shadowy interior of the Mercedes. "It wasn't gonna hurt Jake none. If the movie goes, he gets a good part and he makes himself some bread." He was sweating a bit too heavily to make the atmosphere inside the car very pleasant, and his skin had taken on a grayish tinge. "Boomer wouldn't do nothing to hurt Jake. Me neither. He's our friend."

Friendship apparently has several different definitions. I was so angry I could hardly think.

"Now looky here, Holton," he said. "I can still pull this deal off if you tell Jimmy Yee you made a mistake. You help me and there's a nice fat job doing script rewrites for you. You'll pick up twenty grand or so, I figure. Does that sound like a deal?"

He stuck out his pudgy, sweaty hand, and I derived some satisfaction that now when he needed me he didn't mind shaking my hand. However, I now minded shaking his. I was beginning to understand about face.

"Stop here," I told the driver while Brown's unshaken hand waved in the air. The car slowed and stopped at the curb.

"I won't say anything to Robin Eckhard, because he's well aware of you anyway. And I won't say anything more to Jimmy Yee about you unless he asks me. And as for your nice fat movie job, you can ram it up your nice fat ass."

I opened the car door and got halfway out, then turned back. "And if anything bad has happened to Jake McKay because of you—there's no place you can hide from me."

I slammed the door hard in his face, the loud bang giving me inordinate satisfaction. I was relieved to be out of the stuffy interior of the car and in the fresh air once more, if indeed the air on the crowded and polluted streets of this city could ever be called fresh. The Mercedes didn't move, and I could feel Brown watching me, fearing me, hating me. Being a bully himself, Brown wouldn't know false bravado from the real thing, but I'd meant what I said. If anything had happened to Jake because of Brown, I seriously planned to get even.

Within ten minutes I was in a taxi on my way to the south side of the island and the Aberdeen Yacht Club. It took me a while to explain where I was going to the driver, who spoke no English, but I finally made myself relatively clear and settled back to watch the scenery and to think about Boomer Crane's treachery.

Poor Jake. He'd come to Asia to escape from the politics, the back-bitings, the dirty dealings and the double-crossings of the film industry, and now here he was, and me too, in the middle of a Chinese soap opera. If Boomer Crane was a black hat, could I trust Jimmy Yee? Were Sturdevant and McLoughlin on the up and up? What about Stanley Nivens and his Chinese mistress, Jackie Ho? For that matter, was Kate Longley being one hundred percent honest with me? And was Johnson Lau as concerned as he seemed, or was he going to sail me out into the middle of the South China Sea that afternoon and tell me to walk home. Even Robin Eckhard had tried to chase me off the path of my inquiry. It seemed the only person in Hong Kong I believed in without reservation was Jake McKay, and he was nowhere to be found.

It was a lonely feeling.

It had turned into a great afternoon for a sail, a crisp breeze and warm sunshine in a sky only slightly pock-marked with powder-puff clouds. I only wished I'd known about my sea-going excursion ahead of time because I certainly wasn't dressed for it, being clad in gray slacks, a blue blazer, and an open-necked shirt. But when I arrived at the yacht club I found Johnson Lau had thought of everything and had provided a snug windbreaker for me to wear, one of his own. He also had a pair of deck shoes, which were only half a size smaller than being comfortable.

"We'll take the club's launch, if that's all right, sir," Johnson said formally, taking care to be properly respectful within earshot of the Englishman who sat behind the steward's desk in the club office.

"That will be satisfactory," I said, following his lead.

"You take care, Johnson," the Englishman called as we were walking out the door. "It's going to be blowy out there." Then he looked at me over his glasses, which he wore on the end of his nose. "Not to worry, sir. Johnson's one of the best sailors around here. You're in good hands."

We left the clubhouse and went down one of the jetties to a smart-looking fiberglass power launch moored at the end. It flew the pennant of the club and the Hong Kong flag. Johnson clambered aboard confidently, as if he knew every inch of it.

"Did I tell you this was going to cost you five hundred dollars Hong Kong?" he asked. "I told the boss you were a charter, and the club has rules."

"No problem," I said. Five hundred Hong Kong dollars was only the cost of a good dinner. "You want to tell me what this is all about, Johnson?"

"I will, but I'd rather show you." He started the engine. It was well tuned and in perfect condition. "There's beer in the locker."

When I looked I discovered three bottles each of Asahi, Watney's Ale, Tsingtao and Budweiser. I opened two Tsingtaos and handed one to Johnson as he stood at the wheel, his longish black hair blowing in the wind.

"I figured you for a Bud man," he said. "Glad I was wrong."

We knocked our bottles together in a toast. I hoped like hell he was on the level with me. I really liked Johnson Lau.

I zipped up my borrowed jacket and hunkered down in the stern as the launch made its way smoothly past the breakwater and out into the South China Sea, and I watched as Hong Kong Island got smaller as we moved farther away. I didn't know why I was here or where I was heading, but on a purely hedonistic level I was enjoying the outing. Like most people, at least the ones who don't suffer from seasickness, being on the water was a shot of adrenaline for me.

Johnson held her steady, running south for a while parallel to the long coastline of Hong Kong Island that was almost like a finger pointing to the rest of Southeast Asia. Then abruptly we turned eastward past the village of Stanley on the southernmost tip of Hong Kong. The wind had come up stronger now, and I moved in near Johnson on the glass-sided bridge to find some protection from the breeze. He took out a pack of American cigarettes, and though I had quit some months before, taking one from his proffered pack seemed like a good idea. He handed me his lighter, and I noted it was a Dunhill as I used it and handed it back to him.

"I'm lost," I said. "Where are we?"

"Just south of Cape D'Aguilar and the Shek-O headlands. There's a tiny island group out here called the Po Tois. That's where we're headed." He pointed his finger at some small, hilly islands, some not more than half a mile wide.

"Anybody live out here?" I called to him over the wind.

"A few fishermen, that's all. It's pretty desolate."

As we got closer I noted the islands were hardly fit for human habitation, although there were some places right in Hong Kong about which one might say the same thing. There was an occasional fishing junk with one of those funny-shaped sails that somehow just *look* Chinese, but except for the wind and the occasional plash of an errant wave against the keel it was very quiet. It didn't feel peaceful, though. Maybe because I was nervous and keyed up about what Johnson was going to show me, nothing would have seemed peaceful.

We began threading our way between the islands, some

of which were close enough to each other to throw a base-ball from one shore to another. Johnson navigated deftly to avoid any reefs or submerged rocks. I noticed the tension in the set of his shoulders and the way the cords in his neck were standing out in bas-relief.

He finally turned off the engine and we coasted for a while on the current, squinting into the oncoming gray of the Eastern sky. There was a heaviness in the air, and a still-ness. I don't have much of a sense of direction when I'm on the water, but I figured we had come about ten miles from the yacht basin at Repulse Bay.

We glided past the end of one of the islands and then Johnson's breath quickened and he touched my shoulder and pointed off to starboard with one hand, with the other holding a finger to his lips to urge my silence. I looked in the direction of his point, and my stomach did a triple flip.

There was *The Hong Kong Lady*, lying at anchor in shallow water, in the crook of a natural harbor just off a broad, wide beach that ran to the foot of a heavily wooded hillside that seemed to be all there was of a small island. Part of the racing yacht's hull had been refinished with a cheap walnut stain, and her masts had been stripped, but there was no mistaking the clean, sleek lines of Jake McKay's baby.

Sound carries over water, so I dropped my voice to a whisper even though we were a good three hundred yards from the boat. "How did you happen to find her?"

"I met this bird yesterday on the Kowloon side," he an-swered, his hushed tone matching mine. "My flat is tiny, and she was staying at the Pen with her parents—they live in Dallas. So I arranged a little moonlight sail and a ro-mantic shipboard supper. I borrowed the boat of one of the Brits I crew for—he's in Tokyo and I didn't think he'd mind, or even find out about it, for all that. These islands are great places for bringing a bird—no boat traffic, no one to shoo you away, and it's as romantic as hell on a warm night. And I know this lagoon—it's terrific for moonlight swims or whatever. You can imagine my surprise when I saw *The Lady*." He smiled ruefully. "I turned to and went back to Hong Kong at once. It mucked up what was shaping up into a perfectly good evening."

"Did you go to the police?"

He looked scornfully at me as if the idea was totally out of the question, and I remembered what Robin Eckhard had said about his family.

"Have you told anyone else?"

"No," he said. "There's no one else I'm sure I can trust except you."

I reached out and squeezed his shoulder, accepting the supreme compliment.

"It's up to you what you want to do about it now," he said.

"Any idea who's responsible for this?"

He shook his head. I could tell from the way his eyes were glittering that his adrenaline was pumping as much as mine was.

I went back to the stern to get a better look. *The Lady*'s bow was facing us. Johnson came up beside me, quietly on his deck shoes, and handed me an expensive Minolta with a telephoto lens.

"I thought you might like to take some pictures for your vacation scrapbook," he said.

I nodded gratefully. Johnson Lau was a bright, efficient kid, and he was putting his ass on the line for me and for Jake. I was glad I had trusted him, glad we had trusted one another.

I started fiddling with the camera, setting the focus and the lens opening, and all at once I felt a hard impact and a sudden numbness in my left arm, and I staggered backwards a few steps. It was only then that the sound of the shot reached me.

I sat down heavily and without grace, the hard deck colliding with my coccyx bone, and my brain registered that pain first before I felt the other, searing fire in my arm. When I looked down I saw that the sleeve of the jacket I had borrowed from Johnson was ripped, and there was an ugly red stain spreading quickly through the fabric, and it finally got through to me that a bullet from a high-powered rifle fired from the deck of *The Hong Kong Lady* had just blown away a fleshy piece of my upper arm.

Johnson was flat on the deck beside me, cursing under his breath, and I was glad to see he wasn't injured but had decided, wiser than I, to get down out of the line of fire. Another bullet screamed over our heads; then a third, lower, gouged out a hunk of the fiberglass hull of the launch. He scrambled crab-fashion to the bridge, keeping low and close to the deck, and started the motor. The boat began to move. It had a good pick up, but to me, bleeding and feeling useless and stupid and scared silly, it seemed inconceivable that any boat could move that slowly.

Our unseen assailants fired another shot, but it was aimed at Johnson Lau, now several feet away from me, so the paralyzing whine of the bullet didn't affect me as much as the others had. Thankfully the shot missed him, because I was going into shock. Had anything happened to Johnson, I doubt I would have been able to take the helm and get us the hell out of there.

It took me a while to register that I had actually been shot—something that only happened to other people, or in the movies. The physical damage was nothing compared to the twisting, knotting fear in my gut as I saw blood filling up the sleeve of the white windbreaker and running down my hand and off my fingers.

My arm was hurting terribly, now. I gulped a deep breath and lay back, the deck hard under my head, and drew my knees up to my stomach. Waves of pain and nausea washed over me like a starfish in a tidepool, red waves, and then the red tide engulfed me and I gratefully slipped beneath it and missed out on the rest of my boat ride.

Chapter Seven

Before I even opened my eyes I was aware of the smells—fish, seawater, sewage and kerosene, and then as if to cover it all, eye-smarting incense. I coughed, and forced my eyes open through the Krazy Glue that had cemented them shut. I was on a straw-filled pallet in what seemed to be a small wooden room, a kerosene lamp was burning nearby, and Johnson Lau was talking in Cantonese to a wrinkled little Chinese man wearing black pajamas, the uniform of the Hoklas, the boat people.

I stirred, and Johnson looked down at me.

"You're going to be okay," he said.

The pain in my arm made him seem like a liar. I groaned.

"This is my Uncle Pok," Johnson said, and the old man smiled and bobbed his head.

"At the risk of being trite, Johnson, where am I?"

"You're aboard my uncle's junk in Aberdeen Harbour. Now lie quiet."

A plump old woman came bustling into the room, which I now understood was a cabin aboard a boat, carrying a steaming kettle of something which she put down on the floor next to my pallet. I had a sense of floating, and I didn't know whether it was delirium or because we were actually on the water. The old lady looked at me shyly and bowed, and then Johnson picked up a straw-covered flask and poured something into a Chinese teacup, which he held under my nose. It smelled like low-grade gasoline.

"Chinese rice wine," he said. "Drink it all up, it's good for you." He forced the cup to my lips; the wine tasted worse than it smelled. It made me giddy, and huge dragonflies with fluttery wings hummed in my head.

While I was choking down the vile stuff the old woman took up a knife, probably for scaling fish, and began sawing off the left sleeves of my jacket and shirt. It hurt like hell having the arm pulled at, and I didn't look down at the wound when she finally uncovered it—I didn't have the guts.

She regarded the bullet hole with an attitude right out of the Mayo Clinic and then said something to Johnson, who translated.

"Honored Aunt says the bullet went straight through without hitting bone. She says you were lucky."

"I want to go to a hospital," I said.

"Too dangerous, Anthony. That rifle probably had a telescopic sight on it, and you might have been recognized. They'll be looking for you in the hospitals. You stay here with Uncle Pok for a while."

"They know you too, Johnson."

"Ah yes—but I have friends."

I was fighting a dizziness that came and went like taking the dips on a roller coaster. Uncle Pok brought the lamp closer to my face and I turned away from the acrid smell of it. Then Honored Aunt dipped some clean cloths into the steaming kettle. Johnson stripped off the wide leather belt he had been wearing and stuck it between my teeth.

"Bite on this," he said.

I didn't know why I should until the old lady fished the cloths out of the pot on the end of a long wooden spoon and dumped them on my bullet wound. I never knew anything could hurt like that, and I ground my teeth into the belt while my whole body arched off the pallet in agony.

And then the red tide got me again.

I was awakened by heavy snoring. When I opened my

106

eyes it was just at that precise moment between night and morning when the sun was trying to decide whether to come all the way up or to stay where it was and to hell with the world that awaited it.

I was still wearing my wristwatch, its metallic links scummy with congealed blood, but I couldn't move my left arm enough to see what time it was, so I lay back. My arm ached and throbbed, but felt a lot better than it had, so the only thoughts I had were ones of hunger and thirst.

In a few minutes a figure was silhouetted in the hatchway, and squinting through the gloom I could see it was a young girl, dressed in those black pajamas. She didn't look at me but went straight to a curtained-off cubicle in the corner of the cabin, and after a few seconds I heard the unmistakable sound of urination. When she came out again our eyes met and she covered her smile with her hand and scurried back up on deck, a fairy bug that had flitted in and out without ever touching down.

Abruptly the snoring stopped and I heard voices. In a while, Uncle Pok came down into the cabin, his face puffy and creased from sleep, and went into the curtained head. When he came out I raised up on my good elbow and he scolded me for it and pushed me gently but firmly back onto the straw pallet. When he was sure I was there to stay he went back up on deck.

Shortly the smell of cooking wafted down the gangway to me, pungent and sweet, and after a time the young girl came back into the cabin with a pair of chopsticks in a big bowl of rice noodles in brown sauce. When I reached for them she shook her head and sat down on the edge of the mat and began feeding me. The noodles were hardly a Cream of Wheat breakfast but they tasted good and I was grateful for them, and for the hot tea Honored Aunt brought down a few minutes later. In no time I was feeling nourished and stronger.

After I finished eating the girl helped me to stand up, which I didn't seem to be very good at. I had to concentrate on not being giddy and falling on my face. She danced me across the cabin to the head and held open the curtain for me, gesturing to the big rank-smelling chamber pot on the floor. For a brief moment I was afraid she was going to stand there with me, steadying my elbow. But when I braced myself against the bulkhead with one hand she let the curtain drop back into place and withdrew discreetly. She was there waiting for me when I finished, however, to help me back to the bunk. It wasn't until I had lain back down and she'd disappeared up the ladder that I realized I hadn't the slightest idea who she was or what her stake was in seeing that I was fed and cared for. I later found out she was Uncle Pok's eldest granddaughter, but by the time I learned that I was never to see her again.

I felt better after eating, though my arm still pulsed. For the next hour or so I drifted in and out of troubled sleep, but during my more lucid moments I took the opportunity to think. I realized the men who had attacked me in Chater Garden on Sunday night were not muggers, but rather inept hired assassins who had been sent after me specifically, and I kept trying to ignore the fact that the only person who knew I was visiting the Godown that evening and who also knew I was seeing Johnson Lau on Monday afternoon was Katherine Longley. I didn't want to admit, even to myself, that she might be in any way connected with Jake McKay's troubles, or with mine. But it sure as hell looked that way, and disillusionment roiled my innards.

Finally when the sun was well up and I could hear the chugging water traffic outside the porthole, the sounds of commerce and of people yelling in Cantonese, I struggled to my feet and tottered across the cabin and up the five steps to the deck unaided.

Uncle Pok was alarmed to see me there, and with much shouting and waving of his hands he hustled me back below, where he indicated a wash basin and cloth. I managed to get most of the blood off my hand and arm, and washed my face off, too. I could smell my own sweat, but there wasn't much I could do about it with only a small basin of water.

After a while Pok came back with a pair of black pajamas like the rest of them were wearing and indicated I should put them on. They were ridiculously small on me, the pant cuffs reaching just below my knees, and when he topped off the ensemble with one of those big flat coolie hats with a strap that tucks under the chin, I remembered Noel Coward's observation that in the Malay states they have hats like plates that the Britishers don't wear.

I felt as if I were in a thrown-together Halloween costume, but I realized it was necessary; I was taller than most Chinese as it was, and for me to walk the decks wearing Western clothing would have made me more conspicuous than I wanted to be right then. Uncle Pok seemed pleased with the overall effect and ushered me topside so I could see where I was.

To the untrained eye a Chinese junk looks clumsy and ungainly and it's difficult to understand how it stays afloat. In actuality it's a wonder of sea-going efficiency, and aerodynamically speaking one of the best-engineered boats in the water. Its design has remained essentially the same for several centuries—a high stern with a projecting bow, and unlike most boats its hull doesn't close in toward the stern but simply stops abruptly, as though the boatwright had suddenly gotten fed up and gone home. On Uncle Pok's junk the sails were rotted and mildewed, but in their proud day they had been square, adorning four masts, although some older junks had as many as five. The sails were linen, held flat by long bamboo strips, and were designed like Venetian blinds to be spread or shut with just a gentle tug at the lines. Junks have always been built with separate watertight compartments for safety, a feature not adopted by Western shipbuilders until many centuries later. I wondered how many miles of ocean this venerable tub had navigated before taking up its final berth in Aberdeen Harbour.

The boat was well laid-out, and apartment dwellers everywhere could learn from Uncle Pok's utilization of valuable space. Along the starboard rail on the more or less shady side was a flourishing herb garden, and although I'm rather skilled at the use of herbs in cooking, an art I don't get to practice much because Bill always shoos me out of my own kitchen, I could not identify them when they weren't in clearly labeled jars. On deck near the stern was a cooking area with two well-used woks and a giant stew pot, and what little provender the Poks owned that required refrigeration was kept in a steel chest at the end of a long rope hung over the side into the cold water.

A frame had been erected and a primitive canvas stretched over the aft deck for when the torrential *taifun* rains of spring battered the harbor without mercy, and every available inch of storage space had been cleverly put to use. Over the stern an intricate arrangement of chicken coops, housing five hens and a rooster, had been so constructed that the excrement from the birds fell into the water but the eggs were saved. One of the coops had been set up as a breeder, but at the moment there were no chicks incumbent.

Such facilities were common to all the junks in Aberdeen, and most had resident dogs as well, though Uncle Pok's did not. The dogs functioned mainly as rat-catchers, although I had no doubt some of them ended up in the woks. They didn't resemble any dogs I had ever seen before; all had a wild, strange look to them, as unique as Hong Kong is different from the rest of Asia, and Aberdeen was an entity unto itself from Hong Kong.

From my vantage point on the bow I could see similar junks stretched out beyond the range of visibility in either direction, their hulls snuggled against the boats on either side of them, so that it was possible for a person to walk more than a mile from one deck to another and finally to the land without getting his feet wet. The bustle of humanity on these junks, living, cooking, working, giving birth, and dying, was so dense it made some of the over-crowded neighborhoods of Calcutta or Rio look like the suburbs.

The boat people rarely went ashore for any reason, purchasing vegetables and fresh water from the vendor sampans that cruised these incredibly narrow channels. It was so exotic and foreign an existence to me that even now, much later, my mind can hardly comprehend it.

And yet here I was, all at once one of them, black pajamas and all, because it was not safe for me to walk on the land. I was a water-locked prisoner in a jail without bars, a stationary Philip Nolan, as much a captive as the hapless chickens.

After a day or two, once her innate shyness had given way to active curiosity about this round-eyed interloper on her grandfather's boat, Eldest Granddaughter became a delight for me to watch. Her huge brown eyes danced with mischief and the exuberance of youth during the brief moments she was not working at cooking, cleaning, mending, or tending to the fowl. On my second day aboard, when my arm had relaxed into a dull soreness, on the mend courtesy of Honored Aunt's poultices, I managed to teach her rock-scissors-paper, which she approached with the deadly seriousness of learning advanced calculus.

Thank God for her, because otherwise I would have been bored to the point of insanity.

There was no radio or TV, of course, just a short-wave radio that sporadically squawked in Cantonese, nothing to read, and no one with even a few words of English to talk to.

On previous trips to visit Jake I had learned a couple of Cantonese phrases. One of them was *hai,* which means yes, and I used that a lot on the boat. Another was *jo sun,* good morning, which only worked once a day. I had also learned how to ask for the check, which didn't much come up in conversation, but I did know *ne ho lan,* which translates to "you are beautiful."

I said that to Eldest Granddaughter on the second evening as we were catching a tiny breeze on deck before retiring. Her straight black hair glistened with a blue sheen in the moonlight, and she blushed mightily and covered her smile with her hand, but she knew the way in which I meant it. She was, after all, only fourteen—beautiful indeed, slim and coltish in that irresistible way of the half-grown, with a sunshiny innocence that touched my heart. She had managed to learn my name, and I loved watching her try to bend her mouth and tongue around the unfamiliar syllables of "An-to-ny."

I was also familiar with the expression *gwai-lo,* which the Hong Kong Chinese mean in the same way Mexicans use *gringo.* Its literal translation is "foreign devil," and I heard

Uncle Pok and Honored Aunt use it often during my stay with them. They were very kind to me, and I think they almost liked me. But the expression still held.

Uncle Pok let me know it would be best if I stayed below during daylight hours—a punishing restriction. The days were hot and the cabin stuffy and rank, and I was grateful when darkness fell and I could go topside and snatch a few gulps of relatively fresh air, even though Aberdeen Harbour is hardly one of the world's garden spots. Garbage and offal floated on the waters day and night, and if there was no breeze the miasma almost overpowered me. I felt safe enough aboard the rotting junk, but I itched to be on my way, to get back to a semblance of normalcy, to unravel Jake McKay's problems, and to return to civilization—even though the Chinese think of themselves as civilized and the rest of the world as the barbarians.

Perhaps they are more civilized, at that. What Western family living on the knife-edge of poverty would take into their home a hunted and wounded stranger who couldn't even speak their language to thank them, and tend his hurts and feed him and keep him safe, even at possible danger to themselves? Damn few.

Even fewer would accept their own abject poverty with such equanimity and not spend their lives railing at the gods, the government, or the rich people on the hill. The Chinese simply accept it as their fate—their *joss*. *Joss,* the Chinese cousin of the Muslim *kismet,* is a really good way of accepting and rationalizing that which has to be, and I envied the Poks their faith in it. Like any other religion or spiritual belief, whatever gets you through the day or the night is okay.

Apparently my *joss* called for an extended stay on this smelly old barge, dressed in coolie pajamas and jumping at each unfamiliar sound until such time as Johnson Lau saw fit to liberate me.

My arm was healing steadily—that *joss* was good. The wound was clean, and there wouldn't be much more aftermath than an ugly scar. Honored Aunt's scalding concoctions had evidently contained secret herb and root ingredients that prevented infection and promoted healing, and I concentrated on thanking whichever god had sent me to her. I didn't allow myself the self-indulgent masochism of reflecting on how close I had come to dying.

In the meantime, I was eating bean thread or rice three times a day, my kidneys were working double-time to process the copious amounts of tea I was ingesting, and I was wasting away with boredom, my only companion a fourteen-year-old girl who couldn't even talk to me. And for fear of discovery I couldn't even allow the rays of the sun to touch and warm and kiss me.

I was also thinking about *The Hong Kong Lady*, lying out there at anchor in a hidden bay on one of the Po Toi islands. Whoever had stolen her played rough, and I started to wonder if Jake McKay was still alive. Doubts gnawed at me, doubts about Averell Brown and the Yee-Sturdevant-McLoughlin syndicate and the unabashed exploitation of a friend by Boomer Crane. And Kate was in there too, somehow, which seemed to me to be the cruelest betrayal of all.

On my fourth full day aboard, Honored Aunt slaughtered a chicken for dinner. It was the first meat I'd eaten since coming aboard except for a few scraps of pork in the rice or noodles, and I suppose I should have felt special about it. But I'm a city boy born and bred, and to me chicken was purchased wrapped in plastic, already plucked and cut up. I had never been present at a chicken execution before, and though I made every effort to stay below I was unable to escape all of the horror. Whatever anticipation I felt at the prospect of having meat was outweighed by the fact that I had known my dinner personally. And until you've seen the wattled head of a chicken bobbing around in a cooking pot, you've never really comprehended the full meaning of the teenage slang term, "gross out."

After dinner, when the sun was down but not yet out and the sky was the pinkish-purple color of a three-day-old bruise, I sat in the stern with Eldest Granddaughter while she pointed out to me the darkening clouds over the sea and, with a series of charming and graceful hand gestures worthy of a ballerina or a skilled mime, let me know that it was probably going to rain.

The smell of rain was indeed in the air, mingling not unpleasantly with Honored Aunt's stockpot that simmered over a bed of banked charcoal in an iron brazier on the aft deck. I relaxed in the small oasis of calm at the center of my personal turbulence, almost forgetting my own jeopardy in the warmth of the evening and the pleasure of the young girl's company.

It ended too soon, because she had to go to sleep early in order to beat the sun out of bed in the morning to begin her chores, another link in the endless chain of her limited existence. As she rose I stood up, too, and impulsively hugged the child close before she ran off embarrassed but—I hope—pleased. I had grown very fond of her in my four days aboard her home, and was wondering how much it would cost to send her to college, or even if such an arrangement was possible without being construed as charity and resulting in a loss of face to her family. Uncle Pok had saved my life; according to Chinese tradition that made them responsible for me forever. But I had some traditions of my own, and I owed the Poks a great deal. I decided to see about a small trust fund for the girl as soon as I was once more safe and the Jake McKay business had resolved itself.

Honored Aunt took her sleeping mat forward without a word. During my time aboard she had spoken little, and to me not at all. Uncle Pok had ignored me except to scold me about coming up on deck during daylight or getting in his way. He yammered at me now, shooing me below, which was his nightly ritual, and in my stuffy cabin I crawled onto my pallet, the Pulitzer-winning bachelor novelist going to bed at eight-thirty in the evening.

The family had taken to sleeping on deck, and I felt guilty for chasing these charitable people from their beds. But it was useless to protest, to offer them their own cabin. It was a matter of face. Whether a tai-pan of one of the biggest hongs, a whore in a girlie bar in the Wanchai district, a coolie or a beggar or a proper British policeman, the getting and keeping of face was all-important in Hong Kong. Furthermore, if you gain face while making someone else lose it, you've made a more dedicated enemy than if you'd slept with his wife, stolen his wallet, or spilled soy sauce on his best white jacket. It was complicated.

I didn't fall asleep right away, which I took as a sign of recovery. Since waking up in the boat I had been sleeping twelve hours out of every twenty-four, mostly from boredom and recuperation. But tonight I moved erratically between sleeping and waking, often coming wide awake with the remembrance of what seemed like a nightmare but was reality—getting shot. It must have been at least two hours before I fell deeply enough asleep to have it matter.

At about two a.m. I found myself sitting up, alert, roused by footsteps above me on the deck that were not the soft flip-flop of Uncle Pok's sandals nor the dainty padding of the cloth slippers the women wore. The cabin was dark and the night sky, although starry, provided little illumination, so I just lay there and listened. I heard male voices, one of them Uncle Pok's, and they sounded angry. Then came sounds of scuffling, and Eldest Granddaughter's scream brought me out of my bunk.

A figure was coming down the steps into the cabin, carrying a foot-long metal pipe about three inches in diameter. The deck sounds escalated into those of a major struggle, and I didn't wait for my visitor to introduce himself. I simply put all my weight and strength into a punch that caught him on the breastbone before he had a chance to swing at me. He fell back on the steps, arms outflung, and I chopped him under the ear with the side of my hand. My good right hand.

He went limp and dropped the pipe, and I snatched it up as I vaulted over him and went up on deck.

Uncle Pok was sprawled out astern, his head almost floating in his own blood, and his wife was crouched over him, keening. That was all I saw for the moment because one of the intruders was atop the cabin and he leaped onto my back, driving most of the breath out of me. We hit the deck together, and I dropped the pipe before I had a chance to use it. A forearm was around my neck, squeezing, and I jammed my left elbow back into the ribs of the monkey on my back.

The wound in my arm sent quicksilver spasms of pain from shoulder to wrist and I almost lost consciousness. But the instinct to survive is strong in me.

I managed to loosen the chokehold and squirmed around so my back was against the deck and I was face to face with my assailant. It was the young punk with the satin jacket who'd tried to mug me in Chater Garden, only now his nose was spread all over his face like an overripe vegetable that falls off a truck and hits the pavement. My handiwork.

My arms were pinned in a sort of bear hug so I couldn't hit him, but I reared back my head and butted him with my forehead. It hurt me, but it hurt him worse because I got him on the bridge of his broken nose. He screamed and let go, and I pushed him off me and let him have one in the stomach that slowed him down even more. I was on my feet before he was, and as he scrambled up I uppercut him right on the V of his chin. When he went dancing backward, tripped, and hit his head on the gunwale I wondered why whoever it was who had sent him after me didn't get themselves some hired muscle that knew how to fight.

What happened next I'll see again and again, for the rest of my dark and haunted nights in my most corrosive dreams and during those waking times the melancholy hits low and hard, see it grotesquely distorted as in a funhouse mirror.

There was a third intruder, a bigger man, almost as tall and wide as Johnson Lau, and he had been heading toward me menacingly when Eldest Granddaughter hurled herself at him, punching and scratching and hanging on his side like a baby opossum hitching a ride on its mother. Almost without breaking his stride, he grabbed a handful of her shiny black hair and peeled her off him. Then he drew back his fist and struck her twice with all his strength. Across the deck I could hear something crack inside her, and then he dropped her like a discarded candy bar wrapper. She fell against the bulkhead, crumpled and broken, in a way that told me she wasn't going to get up again, and something way down deep in my core died too, some lambent light in my soul flickered and went out forever.

Blinded with outrage and grief, I charged him with a yell

like a maddened Apache, unmindful of the gunshot wound in my arm that had opened in the struggle and was starting to seep blood again. I hit him in the lower chest with my shoulder and he grunted. We toppled to the deck, scratching and clawing, and my hands went for his Adam's apple. I felt the frantic workings of his throat as it labored to open and suck in the air I was denying him.

He flailed around, hitting my bad arm, and the pain made me loosen my grip enough for him to twist free and begin crawling away from me on his hands and knees. I leaped on him from behind, my pumping knee finding its target between his legs. I threw a half nelson on him and we knelt there together in the stern near Honored Aunt, who rocked over her husband's body next to the charcoal brazier where hot-and-sour soup still simmered. I straightened up, taking the little girl's murderer with me, and deliberately pushed his face into the boiling stockpot.

His scream was liquid and bubbly, and then it died as I held his head under the soup, not even feeling the burning on my hands, and he struggled violently for quite a while and then his body convulsed. I held on until his thrashing stopped.

Still I kept him immersed until the scalding in my hands cooked its way through the pure white rage in my brain and I let go and pulled out. He didn't come up, and I realized that in my incandescent fury I had killed a man with my bare hands.

I had time for neither grief nor philosophy, because the one I had cold-cocked down in the cabin had crawled out on deck and was looking for his lead pipe. Even Satin Jacket was showing signs of stirring. My hands were burned, one arm was virtually useless; I had to get the hell out of there.

One avenue of escape was into the dirty water of the

harbor and, with an open wound, almost a guarantee of typhoid or hepatitis. Another was across the deck, over the side of the boat, and onto the deck of the neighboring junk moored three feet away.

I chose the second, making the leap easily to the great surprise of the boat's owners, who hardly knew what had happened before I crossed their deck and jumped to the next junk, my pursuers clomping along behind me. It occurred to me that being a *gwai-lo* I might be detained by one of my temporary hosts, but I suppose the Hong Kong Chinese are much like the citizens of New York who just don't want to become involved in the problems of others. So I was simply observed as a crazy foreign devil as I made my way across the decks of at least twenty stationary junks before I hit the quay and raced onto dry land in the coastal village of Aberdeen.

I wished I had Boomer Crane's football moves as I raced through the streets ahead of Satin Jacket and Lead Pipe. The streets were fairly deserted and I had a good start, so no one saw me as I whipped around another corner and sprinted into an alley, where I leaned against tattered posters on the side of a building. There was a knife-edged stitch in my side; I am not, after all, seventeen any more. I only had time for three deep breaths before I heard the runners pounding after me. I moved to the corner of the building and jutted out my good arm at shoulder level, and when Lead Pipe came thundering around the side of the wall into the alley I clotheslined him right across the neck. The impact jarred the fillings in my teeth, but his breath gurgled as his crushed throat gasped for oxygen, and he dropped where he'd stood. This time I thought he was going to stay awhile.

That left only Satin Jacket. I had taken his measure twice

before, but I was in no shape for fighting. I began running again, hating my role of fox to his hound but having no other readily perceivable options. I vaulted over a low wooden fence into a weedy back yard strewn with refuse and rotting boards and rat feces, and crouched low until I heard Satin Jacket run into the alley, hurdle his fallen comrade and pass my hiding place only to stop, probably look around, and then go back and minister to Lead Pipe.

I huddled behind the fence, looking down at my left hand, which was warm and sticky with blood again, until I heard Satin Jacket move away in the direction from which he'd come. My hands were beginning to blister, and I didn't even want to think about my feet—I had, after all, been rousted out of bed and was barefoot.

I had no money for a taxi or even a phone call. Crouching in the darkness I listened to rats gambol in the garbage piles for a while until, as my poor little girl had prophesied, it began raining in big corpulent drops. Within sixty seconds my hair was plastered against my head and my black pajamas hung heavily on me as though I'd been swimming in them.

I felt all at once like one of those ancient, fabled explorers from my grade school history books. Intrepid, I had trekked and tracked the uncharted wilderness and had finally managed, without a paddle, to discover the headwaters of Shit Creek.

Chapter Eight

It took me just a bit under four hours to walk from my rat-infested sanctuary in an Aberdeen junkyard to the luxury high-rise where Kate and Jake and Boomer lived in Repulse Bay, a trip of approximately three miles. Since much of it was accomplished in a torrential rain that would have called out sandbag brigades in Missouri, the best minute of it was extremely unpleasant.

I was at least spared the stress of face-to-face encounters. The Chinese may have many customs that seem peculiar to the Westerner, but they are not so silly as to stroll through a downpour in the middle of the night on a road where not so much as a doorway offers any shelter from the chastising sky.

When I neared the village of Repulse Bay the topography changed from rural road to upscale shopping area; still it remained quiet and deserted, like the back lot of a film studio on a Sunday night. The shops and restaurants looked unused, bogus, even non-utilitarian. By now the rain had modulated to a fine drizzle, but I was too wet and cold to care; I had passed the fail-safe point of discomfort some hours earlier.

And then happily, I was there at the building, and that was my be-all and end-all. There was no beyond that; there was only the building—and shelter, surcease, sanctuary, warm and out of the elements.

I entered the elevator with the graffiti-blemished walls and got off at the seventh floor. Kate had given me a key to the flat on Sunday morning, but it was still with my clothes on Uncle Pok's junk. I knocked loudly and heard movement inside, and then Kate opened the door. The fact that she was fully dressed in the middle of the night didn't register on me at once.

"Sorry I'm late for dinner," I said, but the joke was ill-conceived and poorly timed. Just how much so I was soon to learn.

"My God," she breathed, looking at my general state of disrepair. I brushed past her and went inside, and then the young Chinese man who had been hiding behind the door slammed it shut, and when I turned around I saw he had a gun aimed at my heart. I looked from him to Kate and she gave me a helpless, frightened shrug; I saw the deep red lines of fatigue and wondered what kind of nightmare she'd been going through while I had been living mine.

There were two more Chinese men in the living room. One was youngish, like the man with the gun, and was cleaning his fingernails with a six-inch knife. The other was middle-aged, portly, and elegantly dressed and wearing thick glasses. They both looked mad as hell.

The older man said "Mr. Holton. I am Lau Po-Chih." He spoke in clipped English and his voice was a finely honed steel blade. "These are my sons." The two younger men didn't seem to acknowledge the introductions.

"Sit down," he said in a way that made it seem like an awfully good idea. I sank onto the couch, and even the terror of the moment didn't dilute my relief at sitting on something soft.

Lau Po-Chih just stared at me, his eyes black and cold behind the lenses. He was an expert at milking a dramatic moment, and while I waited I tried bravely to meet his stare; it wouldn't do to lose face, even—or perhaps especially—when I thought I might die at any moment. Then he slowly and deliberately raised his hand and applied a stinging backhand slap across my mouth, his jade ring tearing my lip. I resisted putting my hand up to my face, and just let the blood trickle down my chin. I also resisted saying anything.

"Do you know me, *gwai-lo* filth?"

"No."

"I am the father of Lau Kwock Ping."

I didn't say anything—the name meant nothing to me.

"Johnson Lau," he explained.

"Oh," I said, brightening. It was short-lived, as he slashed me across the face again. This time the ring bruised my jawbone.

"My son," he said in measured tones, "took you for a boat ride on Monday. He returned without you late that evening—with bullet holes in his boat. No one saw him again until yesterday morning. A fisherman found him in the water off the Shek-O headlands. He had died badly. With much suffering. The way you are going to die."

I was sickened, more upset with the news about Johnson than at the prospect of my own imminent demise. Kate's face was chalk-white, and I supposed they'd kill her too. I remembered Robin Eckhard's telling me of Johnson's family and their involvement with the triads, and I knew if I didn't try to make them into friends I was in for a long and eventually terminal ordeal.

"Mr. Lau," I said, "I grieve with you. Johnson was my friend—a new friend, but a friend nonetheless. He was Jake McKay's friend too, and he was trying to help us."

"Explain," Lau ordered, light·flashing off his glasses.

I explained. All of it. I even showed him my bullet wound, now crusted over and seeping slightly.

"They must have recognized the yacht club's launch when they were shooting at us. My guess is they found Johnson and made him tell them where I was, because tonight—last night—they came for me. Three men."

And then I recounted the raid on the junk, and when he heard about Uncle Pok and Eldest Granddaughter Mr. Lau made an animal noise in his throat and took off his glasses and covered his eyes with his other hand. He sat down on the edge of the coffee table, and there was not a sound in that room except for his breathing. When he finally lifted his head I saw that he was crying. I realized the enormity of his sorrow, risking a loss of face to cry before strangers.

"Pok," he said softly, "was the brother of my father."

Kate began crying quietly, too.

"He came here from the mainland about ten years ago," Mr. Lau went on. "What the *gwai-lo* call an eye-eye—an illegal immigrant. I tried to help him, to give him money, but he was too proud. He would take care of his own family, he said. He bought that junk with his meager savings and said he was happy there." He shook his head. "I should have insisted . . ."

"Don't blame yourself."

"Be quiet, Mr. Holton."

"We know where the boat is now. We can go to the police . . ."

"No police!" he said, the words like the cracking of a bullwhip. "There will be no police."

He looked at his sons, who nodded back at him grimly. The shudder that ran through me had nothing to do with the cold, wet pajamas I wore.

"Where is the boat?"

"I'm not familiar with these waters," I said, "but Johnson mentioned the Po Toi Islands. I don't know which one. I might be able to find it again by boat."

"This is no longer your concern."

"Mr. Lau, Johnson tried to help me find Jake McKay,

125

and your uncle took me in, a stranger, and cared for me, and he died for me, as did your grandniece. I myself have been badly hurt, nearly killed. I respectfully disagree with you, sir—it is my concern. I've come all the way from Bangkok to make it so."

"Go back to Bangkok, then. Leave this alone, Mr. Holton, you are but one man."

"Let's work together then."

He shook his head. "How does that profit us? We have no need of your help. You are *gwai-lo*. Go away from here, Mr. Holton."

He put his glasses back on and bowed politely to Kate. "You will please forgive us any unpleasantness in your home, Miss. We have no quarrel with you."

Just like that. As if he was thanking her for tea. Formal and correct and full of sub-arctic vengeance that chilled my soul. The three Laus headed for the door. In the entryway, Mr. Lau turned to address me once more. One parting shot.

It was a pip.

"If you go to the police, Mr. Holton, we shall know of it virtually within minutes. And we will kill you."

The door snicked shut behind them, but their essence remained in the room, a tangible presence. We stayed where we were for a long time and then Kate was on her knees in front of me, finally letting open the floodgates of hysteria she had been bravely suppressing during her own long night. She put her head on my knee and wept with loud, moaning sobs, and I clumsily stroked her hair with my blistered hands. She cried until there was nothing left, no more tears, but only the residual fear that, once implanted, never really leaves us but stays on and makes us reflect how close we have come to the edge of the pit.

When she'd finally expelled as much of the fear as she was ever going to, so that all that was left was an occasional involuntary gasp or sob, I lifted her up from her knees and sat her down next to me on the sofa. "Did they hurt you?"

She shook her head. "I thought they were going to. They arrived here late yesterday afternoon. When I told them I didn't know where you were, they got very abusive and threatened me, but they never really hurt me. Then they decided to wait."

"I'm sorry I got you into this, Kate."

"It's not your fault." By way of reassurance she gave my boiled hand a squeeze that almost sent me through the ceiling. "Oh, God, I'm so rotten," she said. "I've just been feeling sorry for myself, and here you're hurt."

"I've been hurt for days. I'm getting used to it."

"Nonsense," she said, all at once the old in-control Kate. She led me to the bathroom and sat me down on the seat of the commode while she ran a hot bath, complete with oils and salts to relax me, cleanse me, heal me and make me smell like a French whore. While the tub filled she brought me an oversized bath sheet and a man's velour robe that might have been Jake's or Boomer's or maybe someone else's.

I lay there in the tub, my Hokla coolie pajamas in a pathetic heap on the floor, and I let the therapeutic hot water torment and soothe my injuries. After a while I spent some fifteen minutes digging gravel and dirt from the soles of my feet. Then I stood, took the plug out of the tub, and allowed the shower to tattoo its needle spray on my head and shoulders, and I washed my hair with Kate's strawberry-scented shampoo.

As I was drying off, Kate knocked discreetly on the door and I wrapped the bath sheet around my middle and let her in. She'd put on her black silk dressing gown and brought with her a box of cotton swabs and some antiseptic, with which she sterilized my various wounds. By this time I hardly felt the pain anymore, just a tingling sensation simultaneously unpleasant and sensuous. Then she went back out and I put on Mr. X's bathrobe and went to join her.

I refused her offer of a brandy. My body was rebelling against the shock and strain of the last few days, and I wanted to stay awake and alert and sort out some of the ideas bouncing around in my head, caroming off one another like bumper cars in an amusement park. She sat on the floor at my feet, one arm resting on my thigh. She'd poured herself a drink.

"Kate. When Johnson Lau called you on Monday and you tracked me down at the Mandarin to give me the message, what did he say?"

She looked puzzled. "Nothing. Other than that it was important he talk to you."

"He never mentioned a boat ride?"

"No."

I weighed my next words, but they had to be said. "And who did you tell I was going to see Stanley Nivens at the Godown Sunday night?"

"No one." Her tone took on that dangerous edge I was beginning to recognize. "What's all this about?"

"That's what I'd like to know. When I left the Godown two men tried to kill me in Chater Garden."

Her hand went to her mouth. "You never told me that."

"It must have slipped my mind. Did you speak to Averell Brown Monday morning?"

"I don't speak to him at all unless it's absolutely necessary, as well you know." She stood up and took a cigarette from the box on the end table. "What are you implying?"

"You were the only one who knew I'd be at the Godown. You were the only one who knew I'd be seeing Johnson Lau the day I got shot. Averell Brown braced me outside the Mandarin that afternoon, and you were the only one who knew I was there because you'd called Robin Eckhard's office."

She snapped the cigarette lighter shut angrily, inhaled, and jetted smoke through her nose. "Anthony, I've just spent ten hours with three angry men who treated me very badly, and I won't be brow-beaten any further. If there's such a big mysterious conspiracy against you, isn't it possible you were followed to the Godown? I couldn't tell Brown where you were lunching with Robin because until I phoned his office I didn't know myself. And I might remind you that Boomer knew where you were because he drove you there."

She took another puff, very Bette Davis, her eyes snapping anger and two red spots glowing rouge-like on her cheeks. "And I had no idea you were going to see Johnson—for all I knew he was simply going to tell you something on the phone. How could I know you'd run around in the middle of the ocean looking for the Island of Lost Boats?"

"I'm sorry, Kate. I had to ask. I'm not thinking too clearly right now. I believe you. But that puts me back to square one."

She sat down again, some distance from me on the sofa. "What are you going to do now?" she said.

"Kick some ass."

She put her face in her hands for a while and then came up for air. "This just goes against my grain. Guns and kidnapping and killing. I'm just a little girl from the midlands."

"There was no way I could have kept you out of this," I

said. "It's bad enough you had to bear the emotional burden of Jake's disappearing. I just wish we'd met under happier circumstances." That was something people say at funerals, but it seemed grimly appropriate now.

"I'm frightened," she said. She opened her eyes wide, pleading. "Stay here with me."

"I can't," I said. "I've got things to do. Besides, they'll know where I am. They'll be coming for me."

"You're going to get yourself killed!" she wailed.

Touched, I moved over beside her and took her in my arms and let her rest her head on my shoulder. The natural perfume of her hair so close to my face was having its effect on me, and when she was between sobs I lifted her face up by the chin and kissed her on the mouth. Her body stiffened in surprise; then she relaxed and gave in to the kiss.

After a while it was more than just giving in, but giving. Responding. It was what I had sensed beneath the icily efficient aplomb. I answered her fire with my own, and after a time she said, "Take me inside and hold me."

We moved into her room, and I finally found out what she wore to bed.

Kate made a lot of noise during lovemaking. Her climaxes were punctuated by long animal moans that began in a low register and slid up the musical scale in a serial glissando to a wild cry that might have signaled intense pain or pleasure. As for me, my aches and problems were forgotten in a fevered, seeking rush, until finally I tumbled into an exhausted and skittish sleep.

We awakened at nine o'clock to the pealing of her bedside telephone. She chose not to answer it, murmuring into my neck that it was probably her office inquiring why she hadn't come to work. Finally the caller gave up and Kate relaxed against me.

We made love again, and then finally she left me to go into the kitchen and make coffee. I was feeling good; I stretched like a cat and then pain shot through my injured arm and I remembered, with the wetness of her still on me, why I was here and what had happened and what had yet to be accomplished because of the tragic events of the past few days, and it finally penetrated my sex-numbed brain that Johnson Lau and Uncle Pok and Eldest Granddaughter had died because of me and that in all likelihood, Jake was dead too.

And I wanted to get even.

Chapter Nine

I knew one thing: I wasn't going to sit there and do nothing about Jake or Johnson Lau or Eldest Granddaughter. That would be akin to retiring from the human race. I'd come too far and gone through too much in Hong Kong to let someone else do my dirty work. I was much the worse for wear, and all I had accomplished was three innocent people dead and everyone in town mad at me, from the police to the Triads to whoever it was that had stolen Jake's boat. There had been no positives so far, if I didn't count Kate, and by God there would be some before I got on a plane and went back to Bangkok and forgot about Jake McKay and *The Hong Kong Lady*.

I just wished I knew what my next move was going to be.

Kate was in the kitchen on breakfast clean-up and I was on the sofa finishing my third cup of coffee when I heard a key in the front door and my next move walked in carrying an overnight case.

"Well hello there, good buddy," Boomer Crane said.

I put down my cup and went over to him, and when he bent to put his bag on the floor I hit him. It wasn't one of my better punches, but sucker punches don't really have to be good, and it caught him completely by surprise, slamming him back against the front door. I took his jacket in my fists and threw him across the living room. He fell over the coffee table and became wedged between it and the sofa, and before he could get up I landed on his chest with my knees, and whatever fight was left in him rushed out along with most of his breath.

I waited until he got another lung full, and slapped him across the face backhanded. He looked up at me without

132

fear, but in his eyes was puzzlement and concern that I could see gradually turning to anger.

The sounds of combat had brought Kate out from the kitchen, screaming, "Stop it this instant!" like a substitute teacher trying to control a class of nine-year-old rowdies.

"You fuck!" I snarled at Boomer. "You set Jake up, didn't you?" I had wriggled up so my knees were pinning his arms to the floor. "Didn't you? Answer me or I'll knock every tooth out of your head."

He shut his eyes in anticipation of another blow. When it didn't come he opened them again and said reasonably, "Let me up, all right?"

I clambered off him. He shook his head to clear it, and pulled himself up onto the sofa. He rubbed his jaw and then took out a handkerchief and spit some blood into it from a gash on the inside of his cheek. "That was a sucker punch, Holton."

"Just a love pat."

"Don't be so sure you can do it again."

I shuddered as I remembered too late that Boomer Crane was a trained killer. "You set Jake up with that fat-ass Brown. He's your friend and you sold him like beef on a hook."

He considered it for a moment. "So what? Sure I got Brown and Jake together. Brown said he had a movie he wanted to do out here and that there was a good part in it for Jake. He asked me to introduce them and told me if he raised any money through Jake he'd cut me in. Who am I to turn down an easy buck? It was good for me and good for Jake, too."

"You're all heart, Boomer," I said, "and because of you Jake might be dead now. So you start talking to me, everything you know, because I'm running out of time and patience."

He licked his lips. "Can I have a drink first?"

"No."

He thought about that for a while. Then he said, "Fuck you, Holton, this is my house." He went to the wet bar and poured himself a bourbon, neat. A little early in the morning for that sort of thing, I thought. Then he turned around and took a deep breath, about to recite. "Okay, this is it. This is all I know—the whole nine yards."

Wherever did that expression come from, I wondered. Nine yards was not quite enough—in football, it was just short of a first down.

"I told you that I knew Brown in Africa," Boomer said, leaning against the bar with the drink in his hand. "I didn't know him real well, and we didn't like each other much, but it never came to anything more than a lot of tough talk."

"Typical," I said.

"One night just before the big yacht race, Stanley Nivens took me aside. He told me Brown had called him."

I glanced at Kate, whose face had gone chalk white. "What's Nivens got to do with it?"

"He's a foreign correspondent, for chrissakes, he knew Brown in Africa, too."

I turned to Kate. "Why didn't you tell me?"

"I didn't know," she said, her voice small. "This was after Stanley and I—stopped seeing each other."

"Go on," I said to Boomer.

"Nivens told me Brown was trying to reach Jake about the movie, and had asked him to talk to me."

"Stanley was Jake's friend too. Why didn't he do it himself?"

"How should I know?"

"Didn't you ask?"

"Hell, no. Stanley said there'd be a buck in it for me and

that's all I had to hear. When Brown laid out the deal for me I told him I'd help him. Jake said it sounded interesting. I didn't see anything wrong with it at the time."

"Did you later?"

He looked embarrassed. "I figured later it was a con job, but by then it was too late. Jake was already hooked."

I nodded grudgingly. "All right."

"Brown invited me and Jake up to their house on the mid-levels for dinner, and Brown took it from there. Jake introduced him to a lot of his rich friends here, including Jimmy Yee, and they started talking big money. After that I don't know a damn thing. I was out of it."

"And about five grand richer."

"Look," he said, "introducing one guy to another is an easier way to make a few dollars than killing people. I saw an opportunity and I took it."

I turned my back on him and stalked past Kate into the kitchen, where I stood clutching the edge of the sink, angry with myself, disgusted with Boomer and with most of the rest of the civilized world. I heard the two of them talking out in the living room while they put the furniture back to rights. I guess Kate was filling him in about Uncle Pok and the night raiders and the fate of poor Johnson Lau.

If I was to believe Boomer, I was still as much in the dark as the day I'd arrived. The concoction just wouldn't jell for me. I slammed my fist down on the countertop. It hurt. Frustration always hurts.

Boomer came into the kitchen and I turned to face him. "I shouldn't have hit you. I've had a pretty rough time. I'm sorry. You want to do something about it?"

"Not now," he said, wincing as he played with the cut inside his mouth with the tip of his tongue. "Maybe later.

Right now I want to find Jake, and I know you do, too. You have plans?"

I shook my head.

"Look, I know these islands pretty well. I can get a boat."

"Anybody with twenty bucks can get a boat. You'll just get yourself shot like I did."

"Maybe," he said. "But I've been lots of places where there was shooting and I haven't stopped a bullet yet. You game, Holton?"

"That's why I'm here. You mind if I ask you something?"

"Depends on whether you ask nicely. If you get physical with me again I'll tear out your throat."

I nodded. "When you drove me to the Mandarin to have lunch with Robin Eckhard, did you tell anyone where I was? Brown, for instance?"

"I didn't talk to Brown."

"Anyone else?"

"Well, I stopped off for a shooter at the Conrad and Jackie Ho asked me how you were doing. I might have mentioned that I dropped you off at the Mandarin. Why?"

My hands started to shake and I put them behind me so he wouldn't see. "How soon can you get that boat?"

"Tonight," Boomer said.

The luncheon crowd had thinned out by the time I arrived at the Conrad International by taxi that afternoon. I went into the bar and sat at a booth against the wall and asked the tuxedo-clad host if he'd ring the public relations office and ask Mrs. Ho to join me, and then I ordered a Bombay neat. The first sip tasted like perfume.

Jackie Ho appeared in the entryway, the light from the

lobby behind her accenting the willow-thin silhouette, those impossibly delicate hips and the long slim legs and the almost tiny, perfectly shaped ass like an upside-down Valentine heart under the high-slit hotel cheongsam she wore. I slid out of the booth to accept her outstretched hand.

"It's nice to see you again, Anthony Holton," she said. "I wasn't sure you were still in Hong Kong."

"I wouldn't leave without saying good-bye, Jackie. Perish the thought. What will you have?"

She ordered an Americano from the waiting bar maid. "So," she said when we were alone, "have you been seeing old friends?"

"Old ones and some new ones," I said. "I saw Stanley Nivens at the Godown the other evening. Did he tell you?"

She smiled a mysterious smile. "He mentioned it."

"You mean he was sober enough to remember?"

"Oh, Stanley might surprise you. He always acts a lot drunker than he really is. It's part of his dashing foreign correspondent image."

"Why didn't you tell me, Jackie? About you two?"

She raised her feathery eyebrows. "I didn't think you'd be interested."

"Is that why your husband left Hong Kong?"

Her eyes widened in surprise. The waitress came back with her drink, and she took a quick sip of it. "This conversation is certainly taking a personal turn."

"Well, it's fascinating to me, Jackie. So tell me—you started up with Stanley Nivens and Mr. Ho found out and took your son to live in the Philippines? Is that how it went?"

I could tell she was shaken by my digging so deep, so much that she didn't have the sense to shut up. "It isn't something I'm proud of," she said, going on the defensive, "but it happens."

"So now," I said, "you're an outcast among your Chinese friends, and the *gwai-lo*s aren't that crazy about you either. It must have cost you a lot of face."

Her pretty mouth became an angry slit, and she held my gaze steadily, her eyes moving rapidly from one of mine to the other. It had finally dawned on her that she was being baited. "Have I offended you in some way, Mr. Holton?"

"I don't know. Have you? Or have you offended Jake McKay?"

"Mr. McKay?"

"All right," I said, "I'm easy. Let's talk about Averell Brown."

"Mr. Brown?"

"Stop repeating everything I say, Jackie. It's not getting you a damned thing except a few extra seconds to think."

She pushed her drink away. "I don't understand what's the matter with you."

"Sure you do. You set me up. You sent me to the Godown Sunday night and then you sicced those two inept, stupid clowns on me when I came out. And you found out from Boomer Crane that I was having lunch at the Mandarin and you put Averell Brown on my trail. I'm just having a little trouble figuring out the reason."

"I don't know what you're talking about," she said coldly. "You've always been very kind to me—I'd never do anything to hurt you . . ."

"Cut the bullshit, Jackie. You're lying."

That one hit a nerve. It took away her face, and Jackie Ho was no more able to cope with a loss of face than any other Asian. I knew that whatever transpired from here on in, she would never forgive me.

She stood up gracefully, the slit in her cheongsam exposing her long, graceful thigh and the darker fabric at the hip of her pantyhose. "I have no wish to continue speaking with you, Mr. Holton."

"I can see why not. How much is Averell Brown paying you, Jackie?"

A smile flickered and died, to be replaced with a look of deep contempt. Then she made an effort to smooth out her features, ever the polite, proper, respectful Chinese hotel employee. "Thank you for your company, sir. Good afternoon."

She moved away from the booth to the host's station, spoke to him in guttural Cantonese, and scribbled something on a piece of paper. Then she was gone with a sinuous whisper of stocking against stocking. When I called for my bill, the waitress informed me that Mrs. Ho had signed for it.

I had to smile. Jackie had saved face after all.

Chapter Ten

I left the hotel and went out onto Queen's Road where I did some fancy broken-field running through the afternoon traffic, dodging one of the old London double-decker trolley cars that worked its way through the Central district, and finally managed to make it safely across the street to the periphery of Chater Garden. I sat down on a bench that gave me a perfect view of the Conrad's main entrance where the bearded Pakistani doormen handed guests in and out of taxis, and watched some young boys take an outdoor class in tai chi chuan, Chinese shadow boxing where the movements are balletic and stylized, requiring intense concentration and discipline. I wished I had that kind of discipline, because I hate waiting, but fortunately it wasn't required of me that day, because within fifteen minutes Jackie Ho came out of the hotel.

She had changed from her black cheongsam into a pair of fawn-colored slacks and a yellow blouse. She seemed in a hurry as she scrambled into a taxi, and she didn't notice me as I ran across the street, flagged down a cab of my own, and told the driver as best I could to follow her at a discreet distance.

We headed down Queen's Road Central, bumping along the trolley tracks, then turned left on Cotton Tree Drive for a bit until we swung around onto Connaught Road past some luxury hotels and the Star Ferry Terminal, and into an area I wasn't familiar with except by reputation, the section known as the Western waterfront. A block ahead I saw Jackie's cab pull to the curb, and I told my man to stop where he was.

Jackie walked quickly into the throngs of humanity on

the quay, past large posters of Mao that had been there long before Communist China had reclaimed the colony, but I wasn't too far behind her. It was one of the few times in my life I wished I was five foot seven, as I tend to stand out in crowds, especially in Asia.

Jackie turned abruptly into an herb shop overlooking the water. Lim's, the sign said in English, and I suppose the Cantonese characters above it said the same thing. I wandered around the area for a while, trying to look inconspicuous, wondering if she'd come to Lim's to report our conversation to someone. Whatever she was doing, I wished she'd hurry. The Western waterfront had been Communist since the fifties, I was the only Caucasian in sight, and I drew my share of resentful or curious stares.

After about ten minutes Jackie came out of the shop suddenly as if she'd been shot from a cannon. She was frowning, so whatever had transpired inside Lim's must have disturbed her. I stopped in a doorway across the quay and watched her purposeful march back toward the street, her head down, lost in her own thoughts. When she got to Connaught Road and disappeared into the surging mass of pedestrians, I'd lost her.

I walked back down the quay to Lim's herb shop, a little tinkly bell above the door announcing my entrance. Inside, the medicinal odor dizzied me. It was not an antiseptic hospital smell, but that of mold and ferment and things that had once been alive that were now dried and powdered.

An archway curtained off by hanging beads was fronted by a glass-topped counter holding about two dozen bins filled with strange-looking dried animal and vegetable matter carefully labeled in a language I couldn't read. The beads rustled and a tiny old man came bustling out, wearing a padded vest over a collarless shirt buttoned up to his scrawny neck. He was frowning too behind a pair of bi-focals. His face was the color and texture of old saddle leather.

"Hello," I said. "I need something for my sinuses."

"No, no," he said. He came around the counter shaking his head. At his full height he came up to my bottom rib. I tried pointing to my nose, repeating, "Sinus, sinus," but he was guiding me none too gently out of the shop, babbling in Cantonese. One claw-like hand clutched my elbow and the other was pointing a bony finger at the door.

Then another Chinese man came out of the back room and spoke sharply to the old guy, who released his death grip on me and backed away.

"May I assist you?" His English was almost perfect. I guessed him to be in his early forties. He wore the same kind of quilted vest as the older man, but sported a narrow black knit tie that had gone out of style in America with Billy Eckstine, and a Fu Manchu mustache and wispy eight-inch goatee. Four long black hairs sprouted from a mole on his cheek.

"I'm trying to cure my sinus condition," I said.

He smiled with all the warmth of a spitting cobra. "Why not take aspirin?"

"I figured you'd have something more effective."

"You are a stranger to Hong Kong?"

I nodded.

He folded his arms in front of him. "I am sorry you are unwell."

I shrugged. "I guess I'll live."

His obsidian eyes glittered. "I sincerely hope so."

The old man began screaming at him, and after a heated exchange, stomped back through the beads. The younger one turned his attention back to me.

"I am Lim Hak Yang," he said. "This is my shop. We don't often have customers who are not Chinese. Occidentals rarely understand the power of herbs. My father," and he nodded toward the still-moving beaded curtain, "rarely meets any—foreigners."

"I know the term *gwai-lo*."

"Excellent. You speak Cantonese?"

"Just a few tourist phrases."

"And you say you have a sinus condition? This alone has brought you to our shop? Often," he said, picking his words with the precision of a lexicographer, "when we leave the place with which we are familiar, we manifest certain physical problems. From stress. Often it is best to stay home— for reasons of health."

"Are you trying to tell me something, Mr. Lim?"

He stroked his beard. "I simply advise you. Free of charge. That surprises you?"

"There isn't much here in Hong Kong that is free."

"Then treasure my advice as a precious gem," he said. "I am sure your—sinus problems will disappear as by magic when you return to your own home. I do not believe there is anything for you here."

I tried to suppress a chuckle.

"Something amuses you?"

"I was just wondering," I said as I headed for the shop's door, "if that's Cantonese for 'get out of town.' "

I walked back toward Central, past the Macau hydrofoil pier with its vast parking lot by day that becomes "The Poor Man's Nightclub" after dark, a street fair where peddlers, soothsayers, calligraphers and beggars offer live caged songbirds and cheap green stone they pass off as jade, cricket cages and chopsticks and pot-stickers and tea and medicinal herbs and every kind of dope imaginable. It was aptly named, a colorful sidebar to one of the world's most fascinating cities.

But the wonders of Hong Kong couldn't make me forget that my friend Jake McKay might be dead and someone wanted me that way, too. At the moment I wasn't really all that concerned with saving my own bacon. I wanted retribution for Eldest Granddaughter. I wanted to count coup on whoever was running the show. I wanted to find Jake, and now I'd showed my hand to Jackie Ho and Mr. Lim, possibly a fatal error.

What the hell, I'm a writer, not a cop from Interpol.

And I wasn't sure I could trust Boomer Crane. But he was all I had, and he possessed the nautical expertise to help me find my island again, and the experience in combat that would make him a valuable ally. If he turned on me, if he was really one of the bad guys, I'd pay for the mistake of trusting him. But without his help I was dead in the water anyway, so I had little choice. Still, it bothered me; good guy or bad guy, I really didn't like him.

I stopped off at Government House and sought out the office of Robin Eckhard.

"Where in hell have you been?" he raged. "Kate called me on Tuesday and told me you were missing as well."

"I took a little trip," I said. "Out of your jurisdiction. I'm sorry, I should have let someone know."

"Bloody well right you should have. Well, I have no news for you in any case. There's no sign of McKay yet, though God knows we're trying. What about you? Find anything?"

I knew that if I brought the police in on the search, if I told Robin about the island and *The Lady*, Mr. Lau would make good his threat to kill me. But I couldn't just sit there;

I had to give Robin something.

"I don't know, Robin. I visited an herb shop on the Western waterfront this afternoon. Lim's. You know it?"

He looked up sharply. "What were you doing there?"

"Just poking around."

He shook his head. "Damned amateur! You poke too hard at Lim's and you'll pull back a bloody stump."

"Herbs are that powerful?"

"Don't fool with me, Anthony. Lim Hak Yang happens to be the head of one of the most powerful Triad gangs in Hong Kong."

"He's in with Johnson Lau's family?"

"Hardly—they're deadly rivals. Just like your Mafia in the U.S., your Gambinos and Geneveses. Every few years the Triads stage their own little mini-war and we'll find strewn bodies in all sorts of interesting places for a month." He examined his perfect manicure. "You've heard about Johnson?"

I nodded.

"I imagine that's what it's all about then. I'm damned sorry about Johnson. He was an engaging young man. And there's no doubt in my mind there will be retribution some time soon. One of the Lims will turn up horribly butchered and hanging in a meat locker somewhere. The Laus have to retaliate. It's a . . ."

"A matter of face," I finished for him. "So it's open season on the Lims and the Laus and you coppers are going to sit back and enjoy the show."

"We're investigating," he said frostily. "And we don't need your help. We also don't need you to turn up dead somewhere. You stay the hell away from the Lims, Anthony. They're vicious buggers, all of them, and they'll swat you like a bothersome gnat."

I left Government House, hailed a taxi, and went back over the peak to Repulse Bay. The sun was taking an early retirement, making the sky the color of flamingos.

At the flat there was tension in the living room. Kate was tight-lipped and angry and not making any effort to talk to me, or to Boomer either. Boomer looked as serious as a lab report that had come back positive, and was busy doing dark and mysterious things with back packs and webbed belts, all gussied up in a pair of U.S. Army green fatigue pants neatly bloused into spit-shined combat boots, and a brown leather jacket with much of the facing worn away. He had dug up a quilted brown jacket for me, and I sighed as I put it on; I didn't like wearing other people's clothes, and I seemed to have been doing that for days.

"You got boots?" he asked.

"No. When I packed for this trip I didn't know I'd be going into combat."

He surveyed my image and found it wanting, but there wasn't much he could do about it. My height makes me hard to fit, and I was sure there were limits to what sizes the soldier-of-fortune catalogs stocked.

There were dark smudges under Kate's eyes, and she was giving me the accusing look of the mortally wounded. I gave her my best disarming schoolboy smile, but I saw at once it wasn't working. She seemed determined to play the little-girl-left-behind role to its limits.

"I don't suppose I can talk you out of this insanity."

"Not while there's still a chance that Jake is alive. It's what I came here for, Kate. I have to do what I think is right."

"Being right," she said, "doesn't make you any less an animal than they are."

Boomer came back out of his room with an Uzi machine gun in each hand. I had never seen one before except in a movie. He tossed one at me and I caught it with a desperation I didn't know I'd possessed.

"We may get shot." The matter of fact way he said it raised gooseflesh on my arms. "But we'll take some of them pissants down with us."

Kate looked appalled. "Where did you get those? Have they been right here in the flat all this time?" She shuddered. "My God, Boomer!" She gave him a look that would have charred paper and stalked into her room.

I looked at the weapon in my hands, smelling the pungent gun oil and that metallic odor that leaves a funny taste in your mouth. "I thought Hong Kong kept a pretty tight control on firearms."

"They do," he said. "But I got 'em anyway."

I curled my finger around the trigger, feeling the weapon's heft. "I've never fired one of these."

"It's easy. You just shove it up someone's ass and squeeze the trigger. Here."

He gave me a crash course on the operation of an Uzi. He had checked them carefully, cleaned and oiled and coddled them in the manner of those men who were always a little more comfortable with a weapon than without one. I had handled guns before, but always as something foul and disgusting, like a turd. Guns are for killing things.

Boomer barked orders at me like my old basic training platoon sergeant. I didn't like it much, but his time in the revolutionary armies of Africa and South America had better prepared him for commanding this operation than had my four years at UC Berkeley and several more years as a Hollywood hack. He wrapped the Uzis carefully in waterproof oilskins and took them down to his car. When the door shut behind him Kate came out of her room.

"I hate you for doing this, Anthony," she said.

"I can't help it."

"It's revenge you want. You and Boomer. You're two of a kind."

"Not at all," I said, discomfited by her proximity to the truth. "I want Jake."

"And what about me? Do you still want me?"

"You know I do."

"Then don't go."

"I have to."

"After last night . . ."

"Kate, one has nothing to do with the other."

She took a deep breath as though the very act caused her physical pain. "Go then," she said dully. "Never mind me. What I want doesn't matter." Another sigh. "Maybe some day again some other man will want to fuck me . . ."

She paused, but I wasn't going to interrupt her little song of self-pity.

"It'll be a long time before I let anyone touch me again."

I zipped up my jacket.

"Either that, or I'm going to let everyone."

That stung me, but differently than she'd intended. "Quit trying to manipulate me, Kate! I'm too damn old to take guilt trips."

She spun away from me, over to the other side of the room, one of those moves that would seem totally unmotivated on a stage. Kate's undeniable flair for the dramatic, which I had now witnessed on several occasions, was beginning to pall on me.

"Face!" she spat. "You're saving face! Damn you. Damn all of you men and your fucking face!"

"Kate, the world doesn't revolve around you. I want to

148

find Jake and help him if I can, and I want the ones who shot me and killed that little girl. Why must you relate everything to yourself?"

"Because I'm all I have!" she wailed, the tears coming once more. "Nobody else can be counted on. Nobody! They always leave!"

I glanced at my watch. "We can talk about this when I get back."

"*If* you get back."

Boomer chose this moment to reappear, coming all the way into the room and looking from me to Kate like a tennis spectator. It didn't take a rocket scientist to figure out what was going on, but he wasn't really interested.

"Let's go, Holton."

I dislike leaving things up in the air. I felt incomplete, frustrated. Like not putting a period at the end of a sentence. Like playing seventeen holes of golf.

Like the whole nine yards.

I wasn't any more certain than she that I would be coming back, but I didn't know what else to say to her that would make her stop hurting so much. So I chose silence. I nodded curtly at Boomer and went past him to the door. He turned to follow me and Kate said to our backs, "I'll never forgive you for this. Either of you."

Boomer didn't even break stride.

Once in the car, we drove quickly toward Deepwater Bay. The truth is, I was scared silly, but I wasn't about to let Boomer know it. It was foolish male pride, but I was determined to see this suicidal fray through to its ultimate resolution. I reflected that perhaps Kate had been right after all, that Boomer and I were more alike than either of us cared to admit.

I've never counted myself among that number of hairy-chested men who enjoy the stink of their own sweat, whose sole purpose in life seems to be the daily reaffirmation of their own manhood. I've been known to cross the street to avoid confrontation, and I forswear blood sports and arm-wrestling in saloons. I've always considered myself one of the gentle people, given to the appreciation of good music and browsing through art galleries and bookstores. My few violent episodes have been forced upon me, and I look back on them with no pride—more embarrassment and even shame. I am basically a man of peace, sensitivity and, I hope, taste.

Yet I know that within me, as with every man, is a secret but unquenchable desire to every so often be John Wayne. I'm uncertain whether it's social conditioning that makes us feel these stirrings or if it's truly inborn, a biological imperative that comes along with facial hair and descending testes. In any case, it's there, and it was certainly manifesting itself in me on this night as Boomer and I headed through the darkness, armed to the teeth and bent on mayhem.

When we'd been driving for about ten minutes Boomer said, "What's with you and Kate?"

"Nothing I want to discuss with you."

"Suit yourself, but you're gonna have to eventually."

"Why?"

" 'Cause I said."

"What are you, her *dueña?*"

"Could be."

"As far as that goes, what's with you and Jake? I hear you had a fist fight a while back. What was that all about?"

He shrugged. "Just two guys. You know."

"I don't know. Tell me."

"We were drinking," he said. "There was this pretty blonde from San Francisco in the Godown. I'd just come back from South America and I guess I was bragging on myself to impress her. Jake started putting me down. For being a soldier of fortune. Called me a baby-killer. So I called him a pussy. Said all actors were pussies because they live life in the pretend. One thing led to another and we went outside and started to duke it out. A bunch of people followed us and stopped it before things got hairy. Jake got a bloody nose out of it and that was about all. It was no big thing, and it was all forgotten in the morning."

"You think everyone who isn't a killer like you is a pussy?"

"Look, Holton, there are winners and losers, that's all."

"What's your definition?"

"Losers like to lose. They set it up so they do. It takes the pressure off. There's never anyone running up your ass when you're lagging dead last. When you win, everybody expects you to win again and it gets harder. That's why some people are born losers." He glanced over at me. "Kate, f'rinstance. She's a loser. But I guess you know that because it takes one to know one."

"Oh?"

"You think small, Holton. You live with your head in the sand about a million miles away from what's happening. You got a little taste of success with that Pulitzer of yours and you ran like hell away from the States where the big bucks are because you were scared of playing with the big kids. You went to Bangkok, a foreign culture where your books would make you the big fish in the little puddle. Then you come here to Hong Kong after Jake and start riding to head 'em off at the pass, and you don't even know where the fucking pass is. You get here and pull a bird

151

who's still bleeding from the last guy and who's an even bigger loser than you, and then get all bent out of shape when that screws up.

"Same with Jake. He don't have the stones to tough it out in Hollywood, so he comes to Asia and buys himself a big fancy boat and eats a lot of airline stewardess snatch and he thinks that makes him a big man. You're both a couple a fucking classics, you ask me."

I didn't point out that I hadn't asked him. "Then why are you doing this, Boomer? You don't even know me, and it's obvious you don't have much love or respect for Jake. Why are you putting your own ass on the line?"

He grinned at me through the gathering darkness. "It's what I do," he said.

Chapter Eleven

I'm not sure how Boomer arranged for the boat, and I didn't want to know. He obviously had resources in Hong Kong, though, because there was a sleek little twenty-two-foot fiberglass launch waiting for us in a *taifun* shelter in Deepwater Bay.

He went through all sorts of preparatory rituals, and my offers of assistance were answered with guttural grunts and head shakes, so all that was left for me was to sit up on the dock with my feet dangling like a freckle-faced kid fisherman in a Norman Rockwell painting. I was still smarting from what he'd said to me in the car. The truth shall make us free sometimes, but more often than not the truth shall piss us off.

By the time Boomer pronounced us combat-ready, it was close to nine o'clock at night. The marina itself was deserted save for a few stray boat boys who had stayed around for a spirited game of mah-jongg. As we boarded the launch, Boomer was being so quietly efficient that it gave me a shiver.

Sometimes life doesn't make a great deal of sense to me, and clearly this was one of those times. I have lived since I was sixteen by two strict rules: first, that I was never going to have a job where I had to wake up in the morning and say, "Oh shit, I have to go in there and do that again today," and secondly that I would never allow myself to be bored. I've managed to get through most of my adult life without doing either. So it was not an outrageous deviance from the norm that found me being launched into a life-and-death situation from which I might not return.

Under Boomer's ministrations the launch motor kicked

over once and began purring, and I felt the vibration deep in my chest. I was grateful for the quilted jacket because it was cold on the water, the seaward breeze not nearly as benevolent as it first seemed, and I hunched my shoulders and shoved my hands into my pockets.

"You have a plan?" I asked Boomer. "For when we get there?"

"We got to get on the island and see what's what. No sense in planning until we know what we're up against. It could be three coolies with a rifle and an opium pipe, or it could be the whole mother-grabbing Chinese army."

"Which do you think it is?"

"I left my crystal ball in my other fatigues, Holton."

"Look," I said, "all I care about is finding Jake. I don't want to blast a lot of people off the planet. I don't want you doing it either."

His eyes were almost invisible in his fleshy face. "Who are you giving orders?"

"You've got no personal stake here. Jake's the important thing. And I don't like killing just for the hell of it—not ants and cockroaches and not people."

"Sometimes you got to."

"Maybe. But let's avoid it if we can. If Jake isn't there we just turn around and leave. Okay?"

"What if he is there?"

"Then we bring him out, whatever that takes. But let's try to do it without any killing. Fair?"

He chewed on his meaty lower lip, his never-give-an-inch mentality making it hard for him to commit to something as absurd as no killing. We peered into the blackness ahead of us; he had cut the running lights so we couldn't be seen. Finally he exhaled noisily. "You really are a pussy, aren't you, Holton?"

"Fair?" I insisted, not even annoyed. He'd already insulted me far past the point of my reacting.

He shook his head in resignation, lifting his eyes skyward. "Okay. Fair."

We traveled another silent ten minutes, and then Boomer instructed me to take the wheel and hold it steady while he unwrapped the oilskin bundles. He had two handguns in his stash, both U.S. government-issue .45 automatics, and he put one of them in his belt and instructed me to do the same with the other. He slid one of two huge hunting knives into his boot with the hilt running up the back of his calf. Since I was wearing deck shoes and unbloused trousers he fashioned one of the straps that had held the oilskins together into a makeshift garter he tied around my shin and showed me where to place my knife so I could reach it with a simple dip of my right hand. He even made me practice drawing it.

Counting the Uzi I now had three different ways to kill. I wasn't happy about it, but this was Hong Kong, and perhaps it was my *joss*.

The Po Toi Islands appeared ahead of us, squat and malevolent in the murky dark, tainted mushrooms floating on the soup of the sea, and Boomer asked me which way he should go. I wasn't sure. I'd only been out here once before, in daylight. He looked disgusted with me, but that was becoming standard with him.

He slowed the engine until we were almost drifting, moving in and out of the tiny scattered islands like a rat in a watery maze. I was grateful for his seamanship if not his company as our keel skimmed over the jagged rocks and soft sandy bottom.

A few minutes and several islands later we hove into view of the inlet from which the shots had been fired at Johnson and me, and we could see the mast of *The Hong Kong Lady* reaching up into the black sky like a flip-off finger. A dim light burned on her deck, and there were people moving about. On the beach a single kerosene lamp illuminated tools, paint cans and a portable stove. Even from two hundred yards away we heard voices faintly across the water, borne on the stiff breeze. Boomer held his fingers to his lips for silence; we'd lucked out in that the wind was blowing from them to us and they hadn't heard the soft thrum of our motor.

Boomer produced a pair of opera glasses from a pack on his back and peered through them. Then he put them down and carefully steered the launch around to the back side of the island.

The island was actually one large hill beyond the beach, its total land mass around two hundred acres, with a small beach running around to windward where the terrain rose up to an almost vertical cliff. As we moved around the island the steep incline became more of a gentle slope until it too became a beach. Two large motor launches were anchored offshore. Up the hill, near the summit, clustered three Quonset huts, World War II surplus from what I could see of them, all looking makeshift as though they had been erected recently and quickly. A gasoline generator ran noisily, supplying the huts with an inconstant yellow light and covering the sound of our engine. Through the windows we could see shadows, movement, people, but from our vantage point it was impossible to tell how many souls were on the island.

One thing was sure—we were badly outnumbered.

Boomer cut the motor and the tide floated us toward the beach until the bow gently bumped the pitch of sandy bottom as it climbed to the shoreline and stopped. Boomer opened a storage compartment under the red plastic bench seat and took out a large wire-cutter. Then he removed the .45 from his belt, laid it on the seat and, motioning for me to wait, eased himself over the side. He waded hip-deep over to the first launch and moved around to the stern where he disappeared beneath the water. I crouched down low, having learned my lesson about presenting myself as an easy target. After a moment his head broke the surface and he visited the second boat, repeating the process. Then he waded back over to me, holding the wire-cutter aloft, and with much dripping, reboarded over the rail.

"Anybody leaves this island now," he whispered, "it's gonna be on our boat."

He took a small, flat can from his pouch, twisted it open, and began smearing black shoe polish over every inch of exposed skin. When he finished, he extended the can to me. As I was working the thick, oily paste into the skin of my face, neck and the backs of my hands, he took up one of the Uzis. Then, with his .45 in his other hand, he slipped silently into the water again, holding both weapons above the surface and making a jerking motion with his head for me to follow.

I took the second Uzi in one hand and my own .45 in the other and eased over the rail into the water, gasping as the cold wetness rose to my crotch and above. We held our weapons in front of us, shoulder-high, to keep them dry, and began moving towards shore, our blackened faces giving us the grotesque appearance of jolly blackface minstrels.

It was about fifty yards to the beach through the gently lapping surf. The soft bottom sand sucked at my shoes, almost pulling them off as I walked. When we hit dry land, Boomer went into a crouch, sitting back on his heels and walking forward that way, glaring back at me until I did the same, the wetness making my pant legs heavy and cumbersome and the strain setting the muscles in my thighs and calves on fire. I had to accept on blind faith that he'd done this before and knew what he was doing, but the writer in my soul that allowed me to stand back and observe my own actions was more than a little amused at the spectacle we must have presented, duck-walking up a steep hill with machine guns at the ready.

It took us about ten minutes to get up the hill, and when we were within twenty feet of the smallest hut Boomer signaled to stop. It was dark inside. He moved to the window, amazingly quiet for such a big man, and peeked in. Then, scuttling back to me like a sand crab, he spoke in a breathy whisper, all air and no vibrato.

"Seems to be a storeroom. Lots of crates, Chinese markings."

I nodded and followed him to the next hut, and we stopped ten feet from the window, close enough so we could see in but far enough back that the light from inside didn't reach us. A cheap radio was playing atonal Chinese music. From where we crouched we could see only one person, a youth wearing a red satin jacket, the swollen and broken nose unmistakable. We edged over a few steps until we saw another Chinese man drinking tea at a crude table. He was big and mean looking, with the biceps of a dedicated iron-pumper, wearing a .38 revolver in a shoulder holster over his khaki T-shirt. We moved again so we could see the third man in the room, and all at once there was a lump in my throat the size of a volleyball.

There was Jake McKay.

A stained mattress was the cot on which he lounged, with a small, worn-out pillow and a blanket, but no sheets.

He wasn't tied up, but there was little reason to have bound him, since the island was every bit as escape-proof as Alcatraz, and in any event he would have had to get by Satin Jacket and the big man.

Boomer moved silently toward the generator, and when I joined him he put his face close to my ear so I could hear him while the generator noise masked his voice from those inside.

"We gotta get Jake out of there."

"There's probably a lot more people in the big hut."

"All the more reason we need Jake. Even the odds some."

Boomer pulled me around to the other side of the hut where the entrance was, my adrenal glands working overtime. He told me to stand there so that when the door opened whoever came out could see me clearly. That was bad enough, but when he took the machine gun from me, I panicked.

"That big Chink sees an Uzi, he's gonna start shooting. Makes too much noise. Trust Boomer," he said.

I'd trusted him this far. If he wanted to betray me he could have dumped me overboard at sea. I stood there opposite the door like a duck decoy on a pond, only taller and more vulnerable. I still had the .45 in my belt and the knife on my calf, but they lacked the soothing security-blanket property of the Uzi. I'd never felt so exposed.

Boomer stooped, picked up a clod of dirt, and tossed it noisily against the door. Then he stepped back into the shadows against the side of the hut next to the doorway. There was a beat before the door opened and the big Chinese stood there silhouetted in the backlight. He saw me, pulled his pistol from its holster, and started for me, pointing the weapon at my heart, and I raised my hands half-heartedly. When he was about eight steps away from me Boomer stepped in behind him hard and fast, his left arm snaking around the man's neck and over his mouth to stifle any outcry, and the squat, powerful body convulsed, his eyes rolling back to show the whites. Then he sank to his knees, blood spilling from his mouth, and pitched forward onto his face as Boomer deftly removed the knife from his back with an almost theatrical flourish. As advertised, Boomer knew how to insert a blade so it went all the way in without hitting bone.

It was a horrifically impressive performance, accomplished with no sound whatsoever.

In an instant Satin Jacket came hurtling out, waving a gun he never got the chance to use, because the edge of Boomer's hand caught him across the throat. He made a ghastly half-groan, half-bubble, and staggered around, his arms flapping absurdly trying to flail breath into his lungs. Then he fell down hard and with finality, though he continued twitching for a few seconds. The blow had crushed his windpipe.

Boomer was collecting their weapons while I was seriously considering being sick, and then a third figure appeared in the open doorway. Jake McKay looked down at the two corpses in the sand, and then he saw me, his eyes bugging in surprise.

"Jesus Christ," he said.

Maybe he'd mistaken me for somebody else.

Before either of us could say more Boomer hustled us into the hut and closed the door. Jake looked from one of us to the other, his face splitting in that little-boy grin we've all seen in the movies, and he threw his arms around my neck in a bear hug, his week-old beard scratching my cheek.

"What in the hell are you guys doing here?"

"I'm beginning to wonder myself," I said.

Boomer took charge. "What happened, Jake?"

Jake sat down at the table. "They stole my boat."

"How'd you get here?"

"I came looking for *The Lady* in a borrowed launch. I knew it was nowhere near Hong Kong so I figured they might have brought it out here. They found me, and here I am."

"Who's they?"

Jake shrugged. "Nobody speaks English."

"How many of them are here?"

"It changes," Jake said. "Usually there's about ten guys on the island at a time, but people come and go a lot so I'm never sure. I know a boat showed up about an hour ago, I heard it."

"Have they treated you badly?" I said.

"That's relative," he grinned. "They feed me, and they haven't tried to hurt me. I can't figure why they didn't just kill me."

"Any other building on the island besides these three huts?" Boomer said.

"Not that I know of. It's not that big an island."

"Don't forget," I reminded them, "there are people aboard *The Lady*, too."

Boomer nodded grimly. "I didn't forget."

"Fill me in, guys," Jake said. "I've been cooped up here a long time. What's going on?"

"I wish I knew," I told him. "But a lot of people are dead. Johnson Lau, for one."

Jake's eyes filled with tears. "Shit," he said.

Boomer handed Jake the .38 he'd taken from the muscular Chinese. "You know how to use one of these?"

"I've used them in pictures, that's all."

"It'll have to do. Let's get even, Hoss."

"Boomer, we had a deal!" I said. "We've got Jake, now let's go."

"Fuck you, Holton."

"The odds are against us," Jake said.

Boomer snorted. "Three Americans against ten or so gooks, I'd say they were the ones outnumbered."

My distaste for Boomer Crane threatened to burst the boundaries of restraint, but I decided to let his ethnic slurs pass. "Let's let Jake decide," I said. "It's his party."

It was a calculated risk, based on my knowledge of Jake McKay. Boomer and I swiveled around to look at him. With all he'd been through, he didn't need this kind of pressure.

"I'm tired—and scared," Jake said, sounding like it. "I just want to haul ass."

Boomer was sweating, entreating. "We can take 'em, Jake. We got surprise on our side. And these." He waved the Uzi.

"Sorry, Boomer. But I vote we run."

The starch went out of Boomer, disappointment etching his features. After all, he'd only killed two men in the last ten minutes—hardly worth the boat ride.

I picked up my own Uzi, enormously relieved that Jake was unharmed. I opened the door a hairline crack and peered out. There wasn't much light, just the half moon and the illumination spilling from the windows, but I saw no one. I motioned to Jake and Boomer and we slipped quietly out of the hut.

I moved around the two men on the ground, not looking at them, and we started down the hill. The incline was so steep we couldn't possibly go down as quietly as we'd come up. My own momentum made me crash around in the brush trying to keep my balance, and behind me I heard Jake and Boomer having the same problem. But we figured speed was more important right now than stealth.

The hill flattened out and the scrub grass became sand as we reached the level part of the beach. I was about twenty feet from the water when the entire area was lit up in a harsh, blue-white glare, and I heard the bark of a rifle. The sand kicked up a few yards ahead of me and I hit the ground in an instinctive infantry roll, cradling the Uzi against my chest. There were two more shots and Boomer grunted an obscenity behind me before he hit the sand with a *whump!* I rolled over so I could see what was going on.

Jake was sprawled on his face, looking around and apparently unhurt. Beyond him Boomer rolled around on the sand, a rent high on the thigh of his fatigue pants through which an alarming amount of blood spurted. From the top of the hill a powerful searchlight pointed down at us.

We were sitting, or more precisely, lying targets.

I raised up on my elbows, pointed the machine gun, and fired, startled at the way the weapon jumped in my hand. My aim was lousy, and I sprayed ammunition all the way up the hill, the brush flying around crazily. Finally the trail of bullets reached the spotlight I'd been aiming for, and everything went dark again, although dots of light danced crazily on my retinas.

When my vision finally cleared I made out Jake scrambling across the sand to Boomer. I crawled toward them, the smell of cordite stinging my nostrils and the metal of the Uzi hot in my hands. Together we were able to haul the wounded Boomer to his feet.

Our reward was, "Run, you assholes! Leave me be! Get outta here!"

Flanking him, we dragged him toward the water, leaving

163

a path in the sand like one of those giant sea turtles who lays her eggs on the beach and then struggles back into the sea before the sun turns her bony carapace into an oven and bakes her where she lies.

Boomer was heavy and solid, not quite a dead weight but not helping us much, either. He was in a lot of pain. I could hear shouting on the hill, and several men were crashing down the incline toward us, but we kept moving until we reached the surf and waded out about ten feet. Several more shots sang around us and made sinister little hisses as they hit the water. I glanced over my shoulder; five men stood on the beach with their rifles pointed right at us, barking guttural Cantonese obscenities. Jake's eyes met mine over Boomer's bowed head.

"We're toast," he said.

I nodded rueful agreement. We turned around to face landward, a bedraggled trio. I tossed my Uzi into the surf and raised the one hand not supporting Boomer's bulk. Jake looked sullen but resigned as he threw down his handgun and held his arms up, palms outward, in the classic gesture of surrender.

The great commando raid was over.

Chapter Twelve

We had been fairly caught, nailed, trapped, captured, and all because of our own stupidity. I kept thinking of the old adage drilled into me in college about the Six P's—Prior Planning Prevents Piss Poor Performance. It was never more true than here in the middle of the South China Sea where two very dumb citizen soldiers had botched a rescue attempt.

My assessment of the situation was that we would be killed, perhaps quickly and without undue suffering.

We were marched up the hill, past the two dead Chinese, and into the third and largest hut, where we were all shoved roughly into a corner. Boomer sank onto the floor, blood jetting from his thigh, his face ashen. It looked as though the bullet had severed an artery and he was trying to stanch the flow with his fingers.

"This man needs medical attention!" Jake said to one of the Chinese, and his response was a backhanded slap across the face that nearly knocked him down.

I looked around the hut. It was furnished with six army cots with bare mattresses and thin blankets, but there was also a large table with two chairs and a filing cabinet. An old-fashioned metal combination safe squatted against the wall. At one end of the long hut, fiberboard walls with a set-in door separated another room from the main one. One of our captors went to the door and knocked and then came back to our end of the hut without waiting for an answer. After a moment the door opened and Jackie Ho came out, followed by Lim Hak Yang. And after a beat Stanley Nivens emerged, too, seemingly sober.

"Mr. McKay and Mr. Holton," Jackie said with a respectful incline of her head. She looked down at Boomer as if it were Sunday brunch at the Pen. "Mr. Crane." Cool. Jackie Ho was cool.

"S'prised to see you here, Holton. Unexpected, what?" Even sober, Stanley talked like he had a mouthful of yogurt.

"Next time we'll call first," I said.

"That's all well and good, but the question now before Parliament is what are we to do with you. Can't very well send you off on your merry way. Know too much, you s'm."

"I want my fucking boat back!" Jake said. "And Boomer needs a doctor." That was the truth. Boomer's face had turned the same shade as those cardboard sheets laundries put into your finished shirts.

"Not necessary," Stanley said, omitting the third syllable. " 'Fraid we'll have to dispose of you now."

It was all so damned civilized and high-tea British. I refused to let Nivens have it so easy. "If we're not back by morning every cop in Hong Kong will be out here looking for us."

"Try not to insult our intelligence, Mr. Holton," Jackie Ho said. "If the police knew about us they'd be here now, and you wouldn't be."

I looked at Stanley. "Why didn't you kill Jake right away, then?"

"We needed him, you s'm. Still do, for all that."

"For what?" Jake said.

"Guns," Boomer croaked from the floor. "Those crates in the other hut. Guns. Automatic rifles."

"Very astute of you, Crane," Stanley said. "Impressed."

Little puzzle pieces started falling into place and interlocking in my mind. To keep alive a few minutes more I started sorting them out loud. "You're running guns from somewhere in Southeast Asia. Bringing them into Hong

166

Kong for the use of Mr. Lim, here. You wanted Jake's boat because it's big and fast and luxurious enough not to arouse suspicion. You're changing the look of it with all that paint so it won't be recognized, but if it is traced, the whole thing comes back to Jake, who conveniently disappears."

Nivens nodded proudly.

"That's very good, Stanley. When were you sober enough to come up with that?"

"I didn't. All Jackie's idea. Smart little fortune cookie, what? I just came up with the guns."

Boomer stirred in his corner again. "Bung Sukarno," he choked out.

Stanley's eyebrows lifted. "You know about old Bung?"

"Heard about it. Didn't know if it was true or not until now."

"What the hell are you talking about?" I said, remembering the former Indonesian dictator. "Sukarno has been dead for thirty years."

Sweat poured off Boomer's face. He was speaking to me but looking at Stanley Nivens. "In 1963," he said haltingly, wincing every few words with pain, "when Britain and the Malay states announced they were going to form the Malaysian Federation, President Sukarno wasn't happy. He wanted to block the Federation, and to do it he needed weapons. He made a deal with the Red Chinese to purchase a whole lot of rifles. Some say over a hundred thousand. But by the time the deal went through, the U.S. Navy was all over the Pacific because of Vietnam, and Sukarno had no way to get the guns from China to Indonesia without provoking an international incident. So he stored them someplace—nobody knew where."

Stanley preened like a peacock. "*Somebody* knew."

Boomer nodded. "Yeah. Stanley here was a young hotshot on the Reuter's desk in Jakarta back then. He and old Bung got along real well."

"The president loved beautiful women," Stanley said. "And I happened to know a few, which kept him happy. It didn't hurt for a young reporter to have the ear of the president of the country. Sukarno wanted me to be his mouthpiece to the Western world. Quite a feather in my cap, what? Getting exclusives from the presidential palace, and being drinking chums with a world leader. Quite heady for a young fellow like me. Bad luck for all concerned. He had to step down in '66."

"And you sat on the whereabouts of these guns for thirty-some years?"

"It was my ace in the hole, you s'm."

"And then," Jake said, "after all this time you finally found a buyer. Mr. Lim, here."

Lim bowed graciously. "The British are leaving the colony now. And the People's Republic will have their own agenda for several years. Transitions are never easy."

"And for your organization to possess such weaponry— you'd become the de facto rulers of not only Hong Kong, but the Asian underworld. Drug trading, black market, alien smuggling . . ."

Jackie Ho smiled. "Your writer's imagination is showing, Mr. Holton."

"And how do you figure in this scenario, Jackie?"

"One gets tired of coolie status in one's own country," she said. "Bowing and scraping to foreigners who treat you like a fool or a slave or a whore. When I took up with Stanley he told me about the guns one night in a moment of alcoholic excess. My Western education taught me the wisdom of seizing opportunities when they are presented."

"You see, Mr. Holton," Lim put in, "Jackie is my own baby sister."

I leaned back against the wall, the tension finally making me tired. "Is everybody in this fucking country connected to organized crime?"

Jake chimed in, "Only the ones with more than one pair of shoes."

"Guns cost money," I said. "I'm sure Stanley wasn't funding this whole operation with his remittance checks. Was the money to come from Jimmy Yee?"

Stanley's eyes sparkled. "And the beauty part of it is—I'm sure you'll appreciate this, Holton—Jimmy doesn't even *know* he's buying weapons."

"I know," I said. "He thinks he's financing a movie with Tom Cruise and Jake McKay."

"Oh, shit," Jake mumbled.

"Then Averell Brown is in on the deal, too," I said accusingly.

"Mr. Brown is not involved," Jackie assured me. "He's just trying to bilk Jimmy Yee out of seven million dollars. He is a dupe, and not a very bright one at that. He'd no idea the money was to be—diverted."

"By your associates Lloyd Sturdevant and Duncan McLoughlin," I guessed. "Marvelous, Jackie. The swindler gets swindled—and Brown takes all the heat from Yee while Sturdevant and McLoughlin bitch that they've been fleeced as well, and while you keep your skirts nice and clean. And all Stanley had to do was make one drunken phone call to Boomer, who's left holding the bag for setting Jake up with Brown. A bit convoluted, Jackie, but very good. My compliments."

Boomer stirred, looking up at Jackie with loathing. "You fucking gook cunt!" he said. I don't know when he'd managed to get the knife out of his boot, but he'd been so busy trying to keep from bleeding to death that no one had paid him much attention. So we were all startled when the knife went flying through the air, and it was only Boomer's weakened condition that kept his aim from being hard and true. The blade took a chunk out of Jackie Ho's arm, then bounced off and clattered on the floor.

There was just a tick when no one moved, like the freeze frame at the end of a movie. But this time there were no production credits rolling over the scene. This time the moment was broken by one of the Chinese guards, who raised his weapon to his shoulder and blew away the front of Boomer's head. The rifle report in the close room sounded like a detonating H-bomb. Only louder.

The sound shocked everyone, who stayed motionless while it reverberated. Then Mr. Lim turned to the quick-fingered rifleman and read him the Cantonese riot act. In the meantime I was busy trying not to look at what used to be Boomer Crane's face, attempting to keep my stomach from emptying on my shoes. The room smelled of gunpowder and blood and death.

I've seen a bit of violence in my day. The forty-eight hours of Cheung Dong, which gave the title to my prize-winning book, was blood and guts enough for any civilian. But the orgy of death I'd witnessed in the past few days was all close and personal. It was repugnant. It violated my soul. And in that moment of despair came clarity, sanity, and I knew that no matter what, I could not kill again.

The man who'd shot Boomer sheepishly handed his rifle over to one of his fellows and picked up Boomer's body with great effort. He finally got poor Boomer into a modified fireman's carry and staggered out the door, leaving an unspeakable trail of blood and matter behind him. Jake, stunned, was staring at the bloody place on the wall where his roommate's head had been.

"Just so we understand each other," I said, clammy with sweat, "I have a knife strapped to my right leg, too. You can take it from me or not. I won't use it."

Lim barked at one of the other guards, who relieved me of my final piece of killing apparatus and stuck it into his own belt. The spoils of war.

Stanley was examining Jackie's arm, cooing over her like a first-time mommy whose darling had skinned its knee. It was little more than a deep cut, clean and superficial. Jackie seemed to have a knack for coming out of things relatively unscathed.

Stanley glanced up from his ministrations at Jake and me and smiled tightly at us. "Damned sorry about all of this," he said, a proper British gentleman to the end. "Never meant it to go this far, you s'm."

"Why, Stanley?" Jake said plaintively. "You didn't need the money."

"Everyone needs that kind of money, Jake. I'm bloody sick of Asia, and I want to go home. With enough money to tell my family to piss off. We're talking millions here."

"Jimmy Yee thinks he's spending those millions on a movie," I said. "What if he has Brown killed for trying to swindle him?"

Stanley shrugged. "Bloody well serve the fat kaffir right."

Jackie had taken a handkerchief from her pocket and was pressing it against her arm. "This is taking time we don't have, Stanley," she said in a voice that was accustomed to command.

"Give us another five minutes, Jackie," I said. "Call it a thirst for knowledge."

"Yeah," said Jake, "it'd be hell to die stupid."

She sighed, martyred, impatient to be done with us.

"Look here, Holton," Stanley said. "You can't tell me you'd pass up a fortune if our situations were reversed. We're not such a bad lot, really."

"Then maybe you can explain why an old man and a little girl were killed?"

"That was a mistake," Jackie said. "But it's your fault. Everything was working just fine until you arrived in Hong Kong."

"Yes, you've rather mucked up the scenario, old boy." It was beginning to appear that Stanley never had a thought of his own anymore, that his drink-sodden brain had finally turned to Cream of Wheat and everything he said or did parroted his mistress.

"And you've run out of time, Anthony Holton." Jackie said something to two of the armed Chinese and they moved toward me. Jake turned and hugged me around the neck.

"God damn it, I'm so sorry. I wish I'd never called you. Oh shit, Anthony . . ."

I kissed his grizzled cheek. "What are friends for?"

The two guards marched me out the door between them into the chilly night. It's funny how calm one can be in the presence of his own certain death, but I wasn't frightened anymore. I had a few regrets, I had lots of books inside my head that now would never come out, but I was almost detached. It just didn't seem important. I'd had a pretty interesting life, and now I supposed I was going to have a rather unique death.

We started down the hill again. They evidently planned to do it on the beach and then dump me into the sea, far enough from Hong Kong Island that I wouldn't wind up floating in Aberdeen Harbour because the sharks would get me before the riptides did. I'd be just another Yank who disappeared in Asia, like all the MIAs from the Vietnam war who were either buried in shallow ditches along the Ho Chi Minh Trail or who had defected or disappeared into the jungle only to resurface with a new identity and open a saloon-cum-whorehouse in Penang.

Maybe I'd come back a better person. I don't believe we are reincarnated as frogs or dieffenbachia plants, but I do believe that Heaven and Hell are right here where we are, like two separate rooms in one house. The room we choose to live in is the one we get, and on our next trip around we reap what we've sowed, which is a more potent motivation to be a Good Joe than threats of fiery furnaces and little red demons sticking pitchforks into your soft places.

Then again, I might be totally wrong, in which case I'm sure I have a pre-paid reservation for an indefinite stay at the Brimstone Hilton with an unobstructed river view of the Styx. Either way, as I went stumbling down that hill, I figured I would know in about ninety seconds.

Then from behind us I heard a crashing around in the grass and there was a new voice, one I hadn't heard before, and my two executioners stopped walking. My momentum carried me down the incline a few steps, then I stopped and turned around to see what was going on. There were now two more men on the hill above us, men I hadn't seen earlier, and they had machine pistols pointed at my captors, who dropped their own rifles and put their hands high in the air.

One of the new boys spoke to me. It didn't sound too friendly, but it's hard to tell in Cantonese. I put my hands up, too, just to be on the safe side. I didn't know whether I was being rescued or simply re-captured.

Now the five of us ascended the hill once more. If Sir Edmund Hillary had been forced to climb Mount Everest as many times as I'd been up and down that hill he probably would have chucked the whole thing and taken his Sherpa guide somewhere warm and cozy for a beer.

When we passed the bodies of the two men Boomer had killed, the guys who were now in control of our little hiking party stopped and said something to the ones from Jackie and Stanley's army. The answer was long and involved and wound up with everyone looking at me.

I didn't want the credit.

They herded us into the big hut again, which by now was becoming rather crowded. In addition to Jake, Stanley, Jackie, Lim and the six other members of their gang, all of whom were standing with their faces to the wall and their hands atop their heads, there were five other Chinese men with drawn weapons. The five of us who'd just come up the hill made it quite a mob.

Among the five newcomers were Lau Po-Chih and his two remaining sons.

Mr. Lau looked at me coldly. "You are a fool, Mr. Holton. Did you and the others think you could do this by yourselves? You were told to let it alone, were you not?"

"I came to help Jake McKay," I said. "That was my priority."

"You see what misplaced priorities can lead to. Your efforts, however, were most helpful to us. You have been watched since we left you last night—and you were stupid enough to lead us here." He gestured with his machine pistol. "Please join your friend against the wall."

I had only one friend against the wall, and I went and stood next to him, my fingers interlaced atop my head. Jake looked at me and grinned. "Long time no see," he said.

"I know. How've you been?"

"Not bad," he said, "all things considered."

Mr. Lau launched into a long speech in Cantonese and then repeated it in English for the benefit of Jake and Stanley and myself. The gist of it was that he wanted to know exactly what was going on and he suggested someone volunteer to tell him, otherwise he would take measures to find out that would be decidedly unpleasant.

I asked for permission to speak, and when it was granted I lowered my arms and turned around very slowly.

"I'm pretty much in the dark myself, Mr. Lau. But I'll tell you all that I know."

Stanley came away from the wall a bit. "Bugger off, Holton! Shut your mouth!"

One of the Lau brothers stepped forward and jabbed the muzzle of his pistol hard into Stanley's kidney. Stanley screamed and his knees buckled. I glanced back at Jackie. She was looking straight ahead at the barren wall, the set of her shoulders rigid.

I carefully told Lau the whole story, from the beginning. It wasn't much, and I omitted some of the more intricate financial shenanigans because I didn't think he'd care. Lau was a pragmatist, top dog of a powerful criminal organization, and I'm sure he understood that occasionally people screwed other people out of lots of money. That was fine with him. He didn't care that Averell Brown had skunked Jimmy Yee or that Sturdevant and McLoughlin were hanging Brown out to dry. He simply wanted to know who had tortured his son to death, who had killed his uncle and grandniece, and he wanted to know why. My story gave him some of the answers.

"Thank you, Mr. Holton," he said politely. Then he spoke in his own language and Jackie Ho turned around to answer him, her eyes like those of a small animal caught in the glare of oncoming headlights. After a while she began to cry and plead, and as she moved closer to Mr. Lau he raised his arm and smashed his machine pistol across the bridge of her nose. The crunch of bone was nauseating. She screamed and fell down, blood oozing through her fingers. Pretty Jackie Ho would be pretty no more, I thought.

And while everyone was looking at her, Stanley Nivens bolted across the room for the door. It was totally illogical; there was no place to run, nowhere to hide, but it was borne of terror and hopelessness, and nobody made much of an effort to stop him.

Two of Lau's men started after him, but before they reached the door there were two sharp reports from outside and something came crashing through the window and hit the floor, smoking. While we all stared at it another missile followed and the room filled with a sickeningly sweet smell. My eyes smarted terribly and I coughed, because every breath I took was like acid eating away at my mucous membranes. There was general pandemonium inside the hut as we all choked and hacked and banged into one another trying to get out into the fresh air.

It was a veritable Chinese fire drill.

I knocked someone aside to get out the door, ran a few steps over the leaves and twigs carpeting the hilltop, and then ran into someone else who looked like a monster from a cheesy 1950s horror film, with two huge vacant eyes and an elongated rubber protuberance that dangled in front of them like an elephant's trunk. In panic, I gasped, trying to cool my burning lungs, until I recognized The Creature as CID Deputy Superintendent Robin Eckhard.

And then I relaxed totally and completely, which is a polite way of saying that I lost consciousness.

It was humiliating. Commandos aren't supposed to faint.

Chapter Thirteen

Every so often there comes a day when the weather is so clement, the temperature so balmy, the sky so lazy blue, and the sun so warm and kind, that their confluence allows you to forget there are such things as traffic jams and famine and income taxes and household appliances that blow out two days after the warranty expires.

It is on such a day you feel blessed to have been chosen out of the vast cosmos to live on this fine green planet. In some parts of the world this condition is known as Spring Fever, surely a misnomer because it can come in any season.

It was that kind of day aboard *The Hong Kong Lady*.

The poor old girl was looking her age, the worse for wear and bedraggled since her partial walnut re-staining, rather like a pinto pony or a person with a rare skin disease. We were at anchor just outside Repulse Bay, far enough from shore to avoid the small boat traffic that dotted the waterways with Sunday sailors, in the throes of my going-away party. We had decided to keep it small and uncharacteristically stag, the only celebrants being Jake, Robin Eckhard and myself.

We were shirtless and barefoot, sprawled out on the aft deck drinking chilled Mersault and allowing the hot sun to bake it out of us almost as fast as we could imbibe it. Jake had asked the Gloucester House chef to prepare a handsome selection of dim sum, so popular as Sunday brunch in the U.S. but a simple staple here in Hong Kong. It was mid-afternoon, and the dim sum was gone—but there was still plenty of wine.

Jake looked fit, considering his recent ordeal. He'd been

getting a lot of sun and had shaved off his stubble, once more looking like The Kid he'd played in all those war movies three decades ago. I don't know what Jake's secret was for staying youthful into his mid-fifties while making a dedicated effort to win the drinking and wenching championships of the world, but he was a living monument to non-clean living. I'd like to think it was because his heart was pure.

Robin Eckhard, half-naked and covered with tanning oil, draped languorously across a deck lounger, also looking slim and fit. Dapper was the word to best describe him. It was unthinkable to believe he'd ever suffered the indignities of a pimple or a booger or intestinal flu. I had no doubt Robin's *amah* ironed his pajamas.

I, on the other hand, looked like the Picture of Dorian Gray. My arm was freshly bandaged, which would make for a peculiar tanning pattern, my hands were all broken and dried-up blisters, and the soles of my feet were vivid with orange iodine. The clown-white sunblock on my nose that matched my hair, which was badly in need of cutting, further contributed to the image of a tall albino baboon.

I lay quietly with my eyes closed, feeling the heat of the sun in every pore. I was aware of the conversation, of the gentle rocking of the boat, and the aroma from Robin's pipe, undoubtedly a private blend worked up especially for him by the tobacconist at the Hotel Excelsior.

In California they would call this kicking back; I thought of it as recuperation.

I squinched open my eyes as Jake re-emerged from below carrying a sweating bottle of wine and a corkscrew, and I watched while he mated one to the other. He refilled Robin's glass and then mine, looming over me, his shadow across my body, the sun behind him turning his blond hair white, and smiled down at me like a proud father whose off-spring is going away to college in another state.

"You're in my sun," I complained.

"I'm going to miss you, you old son of a bitch."

"You say the nicest things. Get out of my sun."

"Bloody hell if I'm going to miss you," Robin said as Jake went back and sat down. "After all the trouble you've caused, I'll be glad to see the back of you."

"Come on," Jake said. "If it wasn't for Anthony, I'd probably be dead."

"If you're passing out the plaudits, I think our friend Kate is in for some, too," Robin went on. "If she hadn't rung up and told me about you and Crane going off to be heroes, you'd have been for it. It was too late for us to follow you, but when she told us about Lau's visit to your flat, we simply added two and two and followed him. We reasoned the Triads would be watching you pretty closely, between Johnson's death and your incredibly ill-advised visit to Lim's herb shop. I just wish we'd arrived a bit sooner. Damn shame about Crane."

Jake took a big swallow of Mersault. In his nearly supine position most of it trickled down onto his chest. "Boomer checked out the way he always wanted to—in action."

I had to concede the truth in that. The mercenary and I had been different kinds of people, and very often I have a tendency to be hard on those whose lifestyles, ideals and values are far from my own. But if not for Boomer Crane, for his guts and foolhardiness, Jake McKay would not now be lying on the deck of his own boat slobbering wine down his chin. I raised a silent toast to him.

Jake said, "What's going to happen now, Robin? To all those people?"

Robin knocked the dottle from his pipe on the side of the

boat and refilled it from a worn leather pouch. "Well, it's prison for Stanley Nivens and the Ho woman, I imagine. Murder, then kidnapping, piracy, smuggling and conspiracy. I imagine Stanley's family back in the UK will get involved, and there will be lots of phone calls and cables and official complaints in the diplomatic pouches, and he'll get off with a fairly light sentence. Jackie Ho's for it, though, and rightly. If not for her, Stanley would never have gotten involved. As for Lau and Lim and their respective cadres, I couldn't be more delighted to have something to nail them with. Money talks, and there will be bargains struck and names named, and their lawyers will make a lot of money, but I'll wager a few quid on some jail time for both of them."

"Let's not forget Sturdevant and McLoughlin," I said.

"They seem to have done a bunker," Robin said. "By the time we'd mopped up on the island and had you all back safe and more or less sound, they'd closed their bank accounts, packed up *The Daisy Dell*, and left for parts unknown. I imagine they'll hide out on some island—Borneo, maybe—until things cool off. Then they'll simply assimilate into Southeast Asia until they can buy themselves new identity papers—or more likely, new respectability. Buggers like that always land on their feet. Then they'll resurface in Europe, somewhere, and we'll find them. Eventually. Interpol has them in their computer, but for now we won't trouble about them."

"Are you going to trouble about Averell Brown?"

"Brown hasn't done a damn thing that's illegal," Robin said. "Thinking about doing a swindle is no crime. We all know he was trying to dupe Jimmy Yee, and Jimmy knows it too. But Brown does have a film project he's been talking up, and no way in hell can we prove that he never had any intention of producing it. Jimmy is a bit put out, naturally, but the money he lost isn't as important to him as if you or I had our pockets picked at a parade."

Jake said, "Jimmy won't prosecute?"

"Jimmy feels more than a bit of a fool. He's been taken by Brown and flimflammed by Sturdevant, and the more he makes a racket about it, the more face he's likely to lose."

I sat up, squinting into the blue blaze of afternoon. "I'm up to here with face, thank you. It's a wonder anyone ever gets anything accomplished in Asia."

Jake squirmed his way up to a semi-sitting position and leaned against the gunwale. "It's not just Asia, Anthony. Asia puts a name to it, but everyone worries about it."

"I don't give fuck-all about face."

"Don't you?" he said. "Well, suppose you're at the bar of the Hotel Imperial in Bangkok. You pull a bird. She's cute, friendly—you buy her a drink or two and tell her the fascinating yet poignant story of your life, and you figure that by midnight she'll be sitting on your face. Then in walks some other guy looking like a movie star, she takes one look, and bingo-bango, you're talking to an empty stool while she's out on the dance floor with his tongue down her throat. And you're devastated.

"Why? You just met her, she doesn't mean a damn thing to you, and there's fifty other birds in the place you can score with. And even if you don't, that should only be the worst thing that ever happens to you. Why do you feel like shit? It's because your dignity has been ruffled, your ego bruised, and you look like a complete schmuck."

"Because I've lost face?"

"You got it."

"Good analogy, Jake," Robin said. "And so saying, Averell Brown would be wise to haul his not inconsiderable bulk out of Hong Kong instantly, because Jimmy Yee is going to want his face back, and I tremble to think how he's going to get it."

"What about Mr. Lau's face?" I said.

Jake up-ended his empty wineglass. "Don't confuse face with revenge. Lim and Jackie Ho have relatives, friends, maybe co-conspirators who will pay for Lim's excesses. Don't worry about Lau Po-Chih's face."

"Lau has more than enough money to buy his way out of the only rap we can hit him with, the illegal possession of contraband firearms. And when he does, the streets will run bloody red, and there won't be much we can do about it." Robin stood up and stretched. "Lau fills a need in the community, like any other crime figure. He's like a vulture. He and his people clean up the rotting meat the police sometimes don't want to touch. In his own way he keeps things running very nicely for us, maintains a certain order. I don't give a damn about his gambling operation or his whores, and I hardly give one for his drug running."

Jake said, "Opium is a tradition in Hong Kong. As long as it's kept within reasonable boundaries the police frankly close their eyes to it."

"And," Robin said, "when the Triads have their internal wars and a few small-time crooks are found dead in some alley in the Wanch, that's just that many they've taken off the streets for us. Lau will likely beat the criminal rap, or at least get off with a healthy fine, and I for one will be pulling for him that he does."

I shook my head. Sometimes my own naiveté amazes me. I took a cold swallow of wine, which was beginning to cut through the sun's heat and make me a little fuzzy. "Jackie and Stanley made a point of keeping Jake alive. Why? Why didn't they shoot him like they tried to shoot me?"

Robin laughed. "You were worthless to them, old man. But Jake showing up on that island was a stroke of fortune for them." He sat down on the edge of Jake's lounger. "You were their insurance policy, old chum. They were going to take you along on deliveries. And on the off-chance you were attacked or challenged by the authorities out on the water, they would have shot you dead and gone over the side, and you'd have been found on your own boat with contraband guns. Everything would be blamed on the Yank ex-pat who was trying to smuggle arms into Hong Kong and got shot trying. Nobody would have questioned it, and nothing could have been traced back to Stanley or Jackie or the Lims."

"How did they get the guns in the first place?"

"I told you at lunch the other day. Pirates. Stanley has known about those guns forever, known where Sukarno stashed them. When he was a young chap he was too dumb to do anything about it, and by the time he got older he was a hopeless toss-pot. But he spilled the beans to Jackie Ho one night, perhaps in bed, and Jackie is one smart lady. She made a deal with her brother Lim Hak Yang, and they hired pirates to ferry the weapons from Indonesia up here to that little island, normally uninhabited. The big trick was getting them into Hong Kong. They needed a boat that had the run of the place, and that meant a luxury boat that went in and out of the harbor without challenge.

"And Jake's was the fastest boat around, except for Yee's. So they set up their little pre-fab village on the island, and one night when Johnson Lau was getting his pipes cleaned, they took *The Lady*. It's damned simple, once you get an overview of it."

"Overview my ass," I said, and settled back down, closing my eyes. And that was all the conversation for about twenty minutes. We chose instead to enjoy the day, the sun, the breeze, and the good companionship of men who had been through a crucible together and survived.

And then Jake ruined it. "What about Kate?" he said.

The words didn't dissipate as words so often do, but hung heavily in the sea air, tangible, out in the open. It was a question I hadn't cared to address. Kate had pretty much kept out of my way since Jake and I returned from the island, treating me as if I were part of the furniture.

I decided I'd have this conversation on my feet. I stood up and went to lean against the gunwale. "What *about* Kate?"

"I think she needs a friend."

"What did she do for friends before I came along?"

"She hid," Jake said. "You're the first guy she let get close to her since Stanley dumped her for Jackie Ho."

"I warned you," Robin said, "but you wouldn't listen to me. Now I think you ought to stay around a bit and try to make amends. Just to be decent."

"Decent?" I snapped, more annoyed than I should have been. "Pretty funny, coming from the werewolf of Causeway Bay."

"We're not talking about me. We're talking about you—and Kate."

"Come on, pal," Jake cajoled. "Make it right. You're in no hurry to get back to Bangkok, are you? Besides, I've hardly gotten to see you."

"Be a good fellow," Robin said. "Stay."

"Stay," Jake said.

I was being manipulated and there wasn't a damn thing I could do about it. "Before saying 'stay,' " I observed in a fit of childish pique, "one should always give the command to 'sit!' "

Chapter Fourteen

We got back to the flat after a good day, at about seven in the evening, sunburned, sweaty and tipsy. Neither Jake nor I were ready to talk about Boomer's absence. As for Kate, she was making herself quite scarce when the two of us were around.

On this evening she was dressed to go out when we arrived. Whether it just worked out that way or if she waited for us to return so she could make a dramatic exit, I didn't know. But my flight home to Bangkok was early the next morning, and if I was going to talk with her at all, it had to be now, even though, coward that I am, it would have been easier to leave her a note on the kitchen counter.

Jake disappeared into his room and I asked Kate if she'd delay her departure.

"I really have to be someplace," she said. "Can't it wait?"

"No, it can't, and you know it. Come on, Kate, unbend a little."

Put-upon, she sat primly in a living room chair, knees pressed tightly together as if she was on a job interview. I sat across the room from her. She had on a rather severe gray suit, frilly white blouse buttoned to the neck, and low heels; I was covered with tanning oil and wearing cut-off blue jeans and an old shirt of Jake's that was too small for me. We were characters from two different plays who had somehow wandered onto the same stage. Her icy look chilled my sunburned skin.

"Kate, we have to talk. I'm supposed to leave tomorrow, and . . ."

"Everybody leaves," she said. "I'm used to it."

She wasn't going to make it easy for me. "I don't want it to end badly. I really care about you. I know this must be hard for you, with Stanley and all . . ."

Her body became rigid at the mention of his name, and I realized that even if Kate and I were to stay together on any basis whatsoever, Stanley Nivens would always make it a perpetual threesome. At the table, in the bed, Stanley would hang around like a ghost that wasn't dead, only in prison or, if he was lucky, banished from Hong Kong to someplace even more remote, living and breathing and polluting whatever Kate and I might have.

I'd been to that limbo-land, too. I had been the haunt-ee, suffering the agonies of an obsession that was illogical and hopeless but nonetheless real. Shadows and memories have a way of standing in the path of the realities, and I knew how many women had battered their wings against the barrier I had erected, behind which I'd lived to keep the pain away. Now I was on the other side of that barrier, the unprotected side, and it wasn't my shield anymore, but hers.

"Please be kind enough," she said tightly, "not to tell me how much you care for me. You've shown me that. You have priorities in your life and I'm just not one of them."

"Damn it, Kate, I came here to help Jake, and I did. He's safe, right in the next room, and that was the object of the game."

"Game," she murmured. "That's all it was to you, a big-shouldered macho game. Well, you won, Anthony. You got what you wanted from me, didn't you?"

"You really don't believe that, Kate."

"Why not? A little adventure, a quick tumble with a willing and available woman. Another notch on the lance of the Silver Knight." Her gaze flicked up to my white hair.

186

"You really ought to color it, you know. You'd look years younger."

She stood up and walked across the room to the window in that Warner Brothers way of hers, and I began wondering why I'd started this conversation in the first place.

"It's not so bad, Anthony. You have no obligations here, no strings, if that's what's concerning you. Don't worry, you don't have to 'do right' by me. I wasn't a virgin."

I recognized the well-constructed box she was putting me in; I'd been in similar boxes before. She wouldn't let me stay, and she wouldn't allow me to leave without inflicting pain. This was Kate's party, and long experience had taught me that the only way out of it was to keep my mouth shut. I went to the bar and built myself a vodka and tonic.

"I'm going home to England," she sighed. "As soon as I can make arrangements. I've had enough of adventure and intrigue and fleshpots and exotic ports-of-call. I've learned I'm just not cut out for them. I'd make a lousy heroine in one of your cheap novels."

That stung, but I didn't reply. A debate on the literary merits of my work seemed out of place.

She glared at me sadly, Our Lady of the Sorrows. And then she fired her broadside. "It's my fault. I trusted you with my heart."

That one did it. "Your trust was conditional, Kate. You've been hurt before, and so you kept your head buried, and when you finally decided to stick it out again, you got hurt again because your expectations were too high. The rest of us aren't here to live up to your expectations. It doesn't work that way."

"Maybe it should," she said wistfully, her face a theatrical mask of tragedy. I suddenly became weary of her.

"I'm sorry," I said, and took my drink back to the sofa.

She stared at me, unwilling to accept that I was giving up so easily and letting her go. She was stunned that I wasn't going to argue with her, to feed her terrible need for being needed.

Finally she went to the door and turned, her hand on the doorknob, to lob one final shell.

"It's a pity, you know? We could have been so good together."

And then she was gone, a pathetic waif in her drab suit, marching out into the night ready for more pain. I'm sure she would have more enjoyed exiting into the streets of Paris like Edith Piaf in the rain. It was strange. With me being a former screenwriter and Jake a film actor, in the end it was Kate who had seen too many movies.

Jake drove me to the airport the next morning, and on the way we didn't talk much. This had not been like our previous get-togethers; we'd come too close to the edge to feel comfortable about it. But Jake had spent his life living up to his don't-give-a-damn image and it was too late for him to change now.

Except life has a way of changing all of us. We learn, we grow, and sometimes we diminish. I think large pieces of both of us had been left on that little island.

When my bags were checked and my flight called and we were at the boarding gate, Jake gripped my elbow hard enough to hurt.

"Damn it, Anthony, I don't know what to say to you."

"I've never known you to be at a loss for words, Jake."

He looked down at his shoes. "You can't say it was dull."

"No, you throw a hell of a party."

"I wish I could write you out a check for a million dollars," he said.

"That would make me lose face."

"Well, what do you say to somebody who's a good enough friend to kill for you and almost get himself killed, too?"

I looked into Jake's blue eyes, youthful as always but today tired and troubled. "I guess you just say *Ciao*—and don't forget to write."

"I'll never . . ."

"Jake, I hate long Jewish good-byes. Come to Bangkok soon and we'll tie one on the way we used to." I threw an arm around his neck and hugged him roughly. Then I turned and started down the jetway, not looking back. I knew we'd see each other again sometime—just not in Hong Kong. If I never saw Hong Kong again it would be too soon.

I worried that Jake wouldn't be okay. Living up to your own image can wear you out, and there were too many memories for him here that could be triggered by a familiar face, a street or building, the pungent aroma of noodles in brown sauce. I imagined Jake would sell *The Hong Kong Lady* and move somewhere else, where the streets weren't quite so mean and the gritty residue of nightmare wasn't spread over everything he touched like a film of dust.

And that's just what happened. Within a year, Jake was living in Sydney, and the burgeoning Australian film industry was delighted to have in their midst such a prestigious American actor.

Jake worked steadily from then on. He never did buy another boat, though.

When I got back, my house on the canal didn't feel right. It was alien to me for the first time. I ached with homesickness, missing my old place on the Marina Peninsula in Los

Angeles, my waterbed, my paintings, my BMW, and even my Hollywood friends, who might have all been full of shit but certainly not life-threatening.

I'd always loved to travel, loved the idea of being a mysterious expatriate, feeding my publisher reams of romance and adventure and foreign intrigue at ninety thousand words a crack, with envelopes bearing exotic postmarks and foreign stamps which my editor steamed off and took home to his kid. It was fun, all right, all glamorous and fast track, the kind of existence many people dream about. But there is no place like home.

I slept in the next morning and needed an entire pot of Bill's hideous coffee to jump-start me. Then I sat at my computer and drummed my fingers on the keys with the power off, staring out at the boat traffic on the klong. I wasn't very motivated to write. I even called the airlines to check the flight schedules back to Los Angeles.

And then I got the idea of turning my Hong Kong adventure into a novel, and my blood started racing. I booted up the computer, slugged down the last of the coffee, and formatted a page.

According to the airlines, it was possible to get on a plane in Bangkok on Wednesday morning at ten o'clock and arrive in California at about ten-thirty on that same Wednesday morning, and I thought idly that if I stayed on airplanes for the rest of my life it might be possible to age only half an hour out of every twenty-four, thus tapping into the secret of almost perpetual youth. That way I could live for another century or so.

I decided it wouldn't nearly be worth it.